MW01641731

LILY

AND THE

MOCKINGBIRD

John Ellington

ISBN: 979-8-9895088-2-2

To Milly, thanks for being my "Samantha".

No one could ask for a better dog and best friend than you.

Prologue

I know this place, he thought—or perhaps said. The words hovered on the fine line between subconscious murmur and fleeting reality, pulled from him through dense, reverberating air. A sense of foreboding settled in, crippling any higher thought beyond observation—though it was the very act of observing that paralyzed him.

The large, triangular stone bore the likeness of a man, draped in sheets of moss so dark they feigned black. To his right stood a single dead hemlock, its limbs heavy and parasitized, stripped of the rich green needles it had in life. Now, it belonged to the spirit world—gray, mottled, forsaken.

His feet moved forward of their own volition, communication with his mind somehow severed. *How do I know this place that I've never seen?* A fair question, but one that was unanswerable. He passed through an opening framed by dense, twisting hardwoods and out into a circular clearing. A mixture of soot and ash clung to the forest floor and to the bases of surrounding trees. *A recent fire.*

A mockingbird drifted lazily down in large, sweeping circles above the clearing until it was only arm's reach above his head. He watched and waited for it to land—but, as he'd somehow expected, it never did. It took no notice of him, never so much as glanced his way. Its wings beat with rhythmic precision, bound to some invisible, silent metronome, as if compelled to circle endlessly—until the moment it no longer had to, though it would never know when that moment arrived.

"I need to leave," he tried saying to the mockingbird.

Circles.

Dread was momentarily replaced by curiosity when he noticed something glistening through the ashes at the center of this half-known place with the brightness of life and hope, sentiments otherwise forbidden by the clearing. *The air is heavy.* He trudged forward towards the object, but with each step his body seemed to become heavier, bearing him down. Before he realized it, he was crawling on his hands and knees, desperate for the glimmer of hope, feeling that he was crawling towards a moment or a mindset more than something tangible.

Brushing the ash away, he finally took hold of the object. His hands burned when they made contact, but not in a way that was unpleasant. They burned with the strange pleasure of hot water being poured over one's head in the shower or in a pool. A burning that heightens your senses and grounds you firmly in the present moment but does no physical harm.

As soon as he picked it up, he knew exactly what he held and somehow realized he had known all along

The locket I gave Lily…

The mockingbird's head finally turned, and its shiny black eyes fixed on him as he found the strength to stand up. Yet, it continued its eternal circular flight, not needing vision for something it had always done. Looking up from the locket, he noticed the edge of the woods taking on a reddish hue.

Something's not right.

The mockingbird opened its mouth and cried, "It hurts the trees. It hurts the trees. It hurts the trees."

The locket suddenly became so cold that it produced a different kind of burn, this one painful and unwelcoming. He couldn't drop it. His hand was closed tightly, ignoring his mind's pleading. Panicking, he looked up, searching for an escape out of the clearing, and noticed the trees. Every scale of bark was outlined by a slow seepage of blood. None were spared. Somewhere deep in the woods, on all sides, a light began to grow. The seep became a torrent as blood flooded toward him from the edges.

"It hurts the trees. It hurts the trees. It hurts the trees."

At once, the blood on the ground caught fire and he was stuck in the middle of an inferno with the bird, still eternally circling.

It called to him again, "You can't stay here, Brenner! You must leave! It hurts the trees. It will hurt you! You must leave! Brenner… Brenner… Bren—"

"—ner! Wake up, Brenner, it's just a dream!"

Brenner awoke suddenly, drenched in sweat and gasping, feeling relieved to taste normal—albeit stale—bedroom air unburdened by the smoke of his dream. He looked over at his wife, mind still struggling to comprehend it hadn't been real. He was safe.

"Was it the same dream again?" Lily asked, stretching her legs lazily toward the end of the bed. She yawned, glancing at the bedside clock—it was 3 a.m.

"Yes," Brenner said, the dream lingering like a shadow. He struggled to understand why it kept invading his sleep. He hadn't told Lily about the locket yet. For some reason, the thought of mentioning her involvement unsettled him—he feared it was more omen than dream.

It was the fourth time that month his restless mind had been filled with bleeding trees and a speaking mockingbird.

"You were gasping in your sleep. I'm not sure you were breathing well. It might be sleep apnea."

"I know," he said in an exhausted, delirious moan. "I am starting to resent falling asleep."

"Maybe you should see a doctor… or even a psychiatrist."

"Yeah." He thought of having to tell a psychiatrist about the locket and Lily. "Maybe."

Chapter 1

Mrs. Williamson had too many cats and she was the only one who didn't realize it. Her husband had a way of looking at the veterinarian that seemed sympathetic but ultimately made his opinion on his wife's obsession with their cats' health painfully clear. No sooner had she bowed her head in anguish over yet another diagnosis than Mr. Williamson turned, intoned a solemn, "I'm so sorry," and punctuated it with submissive eyes and a half-hearted frown—every single time. At first, Brenner misread this expression and attempted some feigned words of consolation. Each time, an exaggerated eye roll from Mr. Williamson sent his efforts straight into the void. Mrs. Williamson was prone to tantrums and required at least five—more often ten—minutes before she was even ready for sympathy.

That left Brenner sitting there with nothing better to do than contemplate what was for lunch. Once, on Mr. Williamson's expected cue, Brenner had let the corner of his lips rise—

subtly enough to go unnoticed by most. Mrs. Williamson was not most. Her gasp of indignation had been almost guttural as she inhaled so forcefully that postnasal drip found its way into her trachea, sending her into a coughing fit.

That's a new one, the young vet thought.

Brenner genuinely cared about the cats, but he was running out of ways to comfort Mrs. Williamson. His supply of well-worn platitudes was limited, and the sheer number of her felines had stretched it thin. Once, he committed the unforgivable sin of repetition. Mrs. Williamson was an older woman, so he'd assumed—wrongly—that she wouldn't remember. The moment he finished saying, "—and we still don't have all the answers, so we shouldn't borrow trouble," she shot up and shrieked, "That's what you said about Whiskers!"

Rest in peace, Whiskers.

"Federal cats", she called them. "You know, the ones that just come around." *Should I correct her?* he wondered, laughing internally. Absolutely not. From that moment forward, Brenner called them federal cats as well, mostly around his largely female staff who quickly accepted the new nomenclature. The next time he stumbled upon a roughened trail with straw strewn about and small patterned dirt circles, he planned to exclaim to his friends, "Those damned federal hogs!" Would they laugh? Likely not. But again, Brenner would.

On April 28th, Mrs. Williamson walked into the small wooden veterinary hospital with a cat that had already burned through eight lives and had at least three legs in the grave.

Just prior to her arrival, Brenner had strolled into the exam room, as he often did when the hours crawled by on the rare slow days. The Williamsons were unloading their burgundy minivan, unbeknownst to him, when his technician, Emily, stepped into the room first.

"I'm so hungry," she said in a whiny voice as she came in.

At least you'll have time to eat lunch.

"Yeah, I am too. What are you—"

"Help! It's Penelope!"

Frantic shouting erupted from the lobby—an unmistakable voice, ravaged by decades of Marlboro Reds. The tone wasn't steady but a strange symphony of tattered notes, strung tightly together to create the illusion of true pitch. If time slowed, it would be obvious that her vocal cords, lacking the strength to hold a note, compensated with a smoky staccato.

"We're here to see Doctor… the young one. The one who looks like a highschooler."

Nice.

"Mrs. Williamson," Brenner called, as he peeked his head around the door frame of Exam Room 2, debating whether he was more offended by her dig at his Achilles heel or the fact that he'd seen enough of her cats to fill the local municipal animal shelter, and she still couldn't remember his name. "What's going on with Penelope?"

She scrambled into the room, her husband lumbering in after her. Brenner nodded at Mr. Williamson—no furtive, unspoken commentary this time. This must be serious.

Then he noticed the labored, wheezing gasps coming from the cat carrier. As an asthmatic himself, Brenner recognized the sound all too well.

Thoughts of a greasy beef patty—dripping with fatty, mouth-coating juices, nestled beneath a semi-solid slice of American cheese that hugged it like a melting blanket—had been drifting through Brenner's mind. Crisp, round, cheek-tingling dill pickles. Crunchy, evenly layered iceberg lettuce. Refreshingly cool yet viscous mayonnaise, mingling with a pungent smear of mustard. All held together by simple yet elegant processed buns.

Anyway, those thoughts vanished the moment Emily and Brenner lunged for the exam table, hastily extracting the gasping cat from its carrier.

As they worked, the now-disheveled doctor caught sight of a small scar on his left hand—the last mark Penelope had left on him.

"Emily, go get the oxygen set up with a mask in the back," Brenner said as he began to suspect Penelope was a short-timer. Emily, ever emotionally unstable, started shaking as she looked back and forth from the vet to the dying cat. "NOW!" Brenner shouted impatiently.

"Oh God! No, don't do this to me! Please, dear God…" Mrs. Williamson shrieked, between gasps. She became weak at her knees and clutched the exam table, melting under the weight of agony.

"Doc," her husband looked up, "You got to save this cat."

Brenner's lifesaving, frantic determination for the briefest of moments came to a complete halt when he heard his client's words. His eyes opened wide, and he blankly stared at Mr. Williamson. A multitude of responses flashed through his cynical mind. *Bob, you have got to bring these dying cats in a little sooner. Why'd you wait until now? I'm not God. What do you expect me to do with this? Etc. etc. etc.*

"Don't worry, I promise we will do everything we can." He gave them both a sincere, compassionate expression as he quickly grabbed Penelope's carrier and whisked her away towards the back of the hospital, where he hoped Emily had been successful in following very basic instructions.

"Did you watch the Braves last night?" an assistant named Stephen started asking when Brenner rounded the corner into the treatment area.

"Not now. Go bring some tissues to Mrs. Williamson and then come to the back and help me with rads. Stat. Where are my Os?" Brenner looked around at a bunch of blank faces.

"I'm getting the mask hooked up now! Sorry, Dr. Johnson told me to feed his post-op foreign body."

"Damn it, Emily! This cat is dying!" Brenner shouted, causing Dr. Johnson to turn around from the surgery table.

"Help Dr. Miles, Emily! All of my patients can wait. Do you need me to scrub out?" he asked Brenner.

"No, I don't think there's anything you can do. Acute respiratory distress in an asthmatic cat. From the way she's breathing, I think she collapsed a lung lobe." He shuddered when he saw the cat's gums turning blue in her panting mouth. "OXYGEN!"

"Here, I'm sorry! Jesus..." Emily said as she dramatically handed the mask to Brenner.

I'll deal with that attitude later. He shoved Penelope's face into the mask. "Hold this still while I pull up drugs. Do not scruff her."

Brenner had almost finished pulling up the Depo-Medrol and Benadryl when Stephen walked back into the room. "Stephen, key in a lateral and v/d thorax," he said, pointing to the X-ray room.

After a few moments of letting the cat breathe 100% oxygen, Brenner addressed his tech and his assistant. "Okay, we need to get her back on oxygen as quickly as possible. On the count of three, you two carry her in there for the rads and I'll push the drugs. As soon as the X-rays are done, put her back on the mask. One… two… three!" The team moved as well as Brenner had hoped. Within seconds, the whirring and "beep" from radiology signified the first picture was complete. "Shit. Well, I called it."

"Right middle?" Dr. Johnson asked from surgery, where he was wrapping up his spay of a 120-pound Rottweiler.

"Yep," Brenner said as he studied the film. The normal black air-filled right middle lung lobe was replaced by a dense shade of grey; a soft tissue opacity signified Penelope had forcefully collapsed the lobe. "Okay, that's enough. We don't need the second picture. Get her back on Os."

"You need to send it," Johnson responded, meaning the cat needed to be referred to an emergency hospital with an oxygen chamber.

"I don't know if she'll make the drive."

"Well, she either dies in the car or dies here. Your call."

"Dr. Miles!" Emily shouted from the X-ray table.

Brenner ran into the room and saw that Penelope had

transitioned to agonal breathing. Her mouth was agape, and she took in deep, rhythmic, labored breaths. In the time it took Wilson to roll the oxygen into the room, Penelope died.

"Son of a bitch!" Brenner shouted, slamming his fist down onto the X-ray table, causing Penelope's body to bounce.

"Can't you do something?" Emily cried, tears welling in her eyes. "Can't we do CPR?"

"What, revive her so she has to die again?" Brenner replied, angrily.

"You have to do something! You can't just let her die!"

"If you want to go to veterinary school, I'll write you a fucking letter of recommendation. Until then, let me do my job." This remark cut Emily deeply, as she had just recently found out she had not been accepted to vet school this application cycle. Brenner had not known this, but even still his comment was cold and uncharacteristic. She left the room in a hurry, tail tucked between her legs. Brenner immediately felt regret and wished he could muster an appropriate apology, but the part of his brain that stored up compassion had been exhausted; he had only enough kindness to keep himself moving forward, and even that was running thin of late.

"You couldn't have done anything differently," Dr. Johnson said firmly, as he took his surgical gloves off.

"That doesn't change the fact I have to go tell the Williamsons."

"They should have brought her sooner," Johnson replied.

"That cat subsisted on a diet of cheap kibble, dirty water, and cigarette smoke. It's a miracle it stayed alive until now."

"See, exactly. You can't blame yourself."

"I'm tired, Ben. Everything in the last two weeks just keeps dying. I lay awake every night replaying cases, wondering what I could have done differently."

Dr. Johnson walked over and put a hand on each of Brenner's shoulders, looking him kindly, but firmly in the eyes. "Nothing, Miles. You did exactly what I would have done. Sometimes it just goes that way. We can't play God." He studied Brenner's face and realized his words weren't helping. "Are you and Lily still going camping this weekend?"

Brenner's face lit up for the first time in days and he checked his watch, seeing it was fifteen minutes past four. "Hell yeah, brother. This time tomorrow we will be sitting around a campfire, listening to a mountain brook, sipping on whiskey." He even smiled.

"Good. You need to clear your mind. Do you want me to go with you to talk to the Williamsons?"

"No, I got it. I also saw a possible foreign body in the stack next." Brenner's momentary happiness vanished, and his face fell.

"I'll take it. I'm on a roll with foreign bodies, and you've had a busy enough day."

"What did I do to deserve you?" Brenner asked, feeling the massive weight of a multiple-hour surgery that he had been anticipating lift off his shoulders.

Chapter 2

The conversation with the Williamsons went as poorly as expected for Brenner, further eating away at his emotional reserves. He finally left the office just after six, when Ben insisted on taking the last two cases—including a two-year-old Pitt mix presenting with vomiting, diarrhea, inappetence, and lethargy, who had a habit of eating rope.

As he started the engine of his silver Toyota 4Runner, Brenner marveled at Ben's mental fortitude—seemingly unfazed by days that felt endless.

Prior to Brenner's hiring, Dr. Johnson had been the sole veterinarian at the hospital and was on call every weeknight and both days of every weekend. On top of that, Ben's wife, Lisa, had just given birth to their second daughter. Intellectually, Brenner knew that he was feeling compassion fatigue, a condition often warned of in veterinary training. He used to roll his eyes in vet school when some grey-haired professor would ramble on about suicide statistics and the mental toll of performing euthanasia.

Now, however, Brenner understood what the professor had been warning them about. The only thing that staved off full-blown depression was the realization that Dr. Johnson seemed immune to the darkness. If he was mentally strong enough for the job, Brenner was determined to hang in there, too.

***

Lilith Miles, Lily, sat at home awaiting her husband's return. The clock on the stove blinked 3:30. Since she had been too lazy to reset it after the last lightning-induced power outage, she did quick math to arrive at the conclusion it was about 6:30. Although the clinic's hours were nominally 8 a.m. to 5 p.m., Brenner rarely walked through the door of their modest red brick home before 7:30 in the evening. "One more hour," she said aloud to the yawning, stretching Bluetick Coonhound, Samantha, who lay in an old, worn-out dog bed next to the gas fireplace. A feeling of dread passed over Lily when she received the confirmation email on her phone regarding the concert ticket she had just purchased for the following day.

The oven chirped, announcing the preheat cycle was over and she slid the frozen pizza onto the second rack, enjoying the brief exhalation of heat from the stainless-steel appliance. Lily thought about her life, as she often did, waiting alone at home for her husband's return, trying not to anticipate whatever battered, broken emotional condition he was likely in. As if to say she wasn't alone, Sam sleepily lumbered over to the barstool and pushed her nose under Lily's hand. Lily smiled and stroked the dog's soft head, gently sliding a velvety ear through her hand. She envied the dog, while watching its tail start swinging back and forth. Sam ate, played, and slept, and never concerned herself with the encumbering, mind-swamping stress that accompanied life as an adult.

Lily had two dreams in life, both involving children. From an early age, she had set her heart firmly on the idea of being an elementary school teacher. Hanging out with her six younger cousins had brought her more joy than her own family, as she was an only child. The heart tends to want what it's been deprived of, and she felt deprived of siblings, especially younger siblings. She wanted to be a role model and, quite honestly, have someone to mold and gift with wisdom. Some may say it's presumptuous to assume one's own wisdom, but Lily sensed wisdom was simply a function of time spent on Earth. Therefore, as an older sister, she would have precious morsels of sage advice to bestow upon a younger sibling, or two, or three. Her parents had started procreating later in life, as often is the case with professionals, and thus she had no siblings.

"I don't want to be raising a teenager when I'm in my sixties," her father would say when she asked about a brother or sister. A reasonable stance, and one that convinced her to pursue a career as a teacher where she would get to shape many young minds.

Her other dream was to be a mother—for reasons that felt self-evident. From an early age, she had read in the Bible that the Lord wished for His people to "fill their quivers," a call to have many children. She clung to that idea, dreaming of motherhood each night as she drifted to sleep in college, and later during her engagement to Brenner, whom she believed would make a wonderful father.

Her heartbreak had been immeasurable the day she walked out of Dr. Poole's office. He was a highly recommended fertility specialist, praised by those of her friends who valued timeless ideals like family and childbearing—likely half of them. The rest embraced a freer spirit, favoring independence from men and the pleasures of a carefree life—at least outside the walls of a bedroom.

"I'm so sorry, Lily, but it's not going to be possible for you to bring a child to term," he had told her as Brenner held her hand, a hand which began shaking, gently at first, but progressing to an almost uncontrollable convulsion. In a weird way, Lily felt she had lost a child, only one that was never realized.

She was stronger than she knew and channeled that energy into the dream she could control; she was a phenomenal teacher. She had made a name for herself in the small community and parents would petition the school if their children were not selected to be in her class. As their "big sister", Lily took the time to understand each and every one of her students at the core of who they were as people. The fourth-grade year spent in Mrs. Miles's class was transformative to numerous young, developing minds, especially those who had troubled upbringings in broken homes. She showed them the meaning of family and love, the backdrops to her more mundane lessons on math, science, and history. Though her students might forget parts of the multiplication table, they would never forget what it felt like to be loved, and that's what matters, she thought. Her job fulfilled her in a way her lonely home life never could.

Teaching was not her only way of keeping her dream alive. After processing and recovering from Dr. Poole's news, she and Brenner had decided they would pursue surrogacy. Sure, it was expensive, but they both had jobs. Brenner also worked on partial commission at the clinic, meaning an increased case load would directly correlate with a larger paycheck. Once they decided to save for a surrogate, Brenner made it his goal to take as many cases as possible, including a higher percentage of surgical patients.

Since it would take a few years to save up the money, Brenner and Lily decided they would bide their time and practice parenthood by getting a dog. Brenner had lost his childhood dog, Molly, during their engagement, and they had always discussed getting one together, but they worried trying to raise a child and a puppy at the same time would be difficult. Since a child would have to wait, they turned their attention towards finding the precious Bluetick Coonhound puppy, Samantha.

***

Lily started to smell the cheap, grocery store-brand pizza heating from the other side of the kitchen and became suddenly sad. She used to cook, spending hours each week planning extravagant meals, excitedly hurrying to the store to pick the freshest ingredients for quinoa salad, stuffed chicken breast, pan-seared trout. The first few years of marriage tricked her, like so many young lovers, into believing the raw, unfiltered, optimistic motivation would persist indefinitely. She was so madly in love with Brenner that she wanted to shower him with her affection—delicious meals being one of the primary expressions of her passion.

Over the last year, with his late nights at the clinic and the quiet of the empty house, the meals became less special, and the time in preparation became arduous, burdensome, and not the least bit enjoyable. The slothfulness of the human condition took hold of her soul, but not at once. It crept up on her, so insidiously that she barely noticed her chicken piccata regressing to frozen pizza. She seemed to realize it now, sitting alone in the kitchen with the wagging dog, as if someone slapped her in the face with the rock-hard dinner she had just pulled from their overflowing freezer.

It wasn't her fault, though, she told herself. Brenner was barely around, and when he would finally collapse through the door, she was left to pick up the pieces of his fractured soul. She feared she missed parts of him along the way and her husband was now merely a shoddily put together shell of the youthful, hopeful, vivacious man she married three years prior. She had recently taken to praying, since she was running out of things to say to Brenner. No matter how she pleaded, he wouldn't go to therapy. He considered therapy a crutch to the weak and he was strong. *Sure*, she thought, *so strong*.

Brenner vehemently defended his long hours and extra shifts at the clinic any time she mentioned his absence at home. After all, the reason he was working so much was to save up for her dream. If anything, it allowed resentment to find its way into their marriage.

"This is all normal," her mother had told her at breakfast that morning. "You are just out of the honeymoon phase, and you are figuring out how to really be adults together. Your father and I went through the same thing seven years into our marriage." Lily hoped that was true, but she questioned why she and Brenner arrived at this depressing stage after only three years. And there was also her wandering gaze. In the last few months, she felt her eyes pulled to other men, in a way they hadn't since before she met Brenner. She would never do anything, she told herself, but even the temptation scared her. She wondered if having children would ground her and pull her heart closer to Brenner's as his role transformed from an exhausted husband to a loving father.

She jolted when the back door of the house swung open, signifying the somewhat early return of her man. Next, she heard the ceremonious cracking and hiss of a beer can pulled from the fridge that had lived in their mudroom since before they bought the house. He made his way into the kitchen, smiling when he saw his wife. With the Coors Light still in his right hand, he playfully bounded to her and lifted her off the stool into the air.

"It's the weekend! I am free!" Brenner swung Lily in a circle and carried her to the couch, laying her down gently onto her back, where he started kissing her. Lily had anticipated sex since it was Friday. Like many married couples, Lily and Brenner's sex life was stripped of its original spark of spontaneity, and reduced to an almost scheduled task, one that Lily rarely sought out. The diagnosis of infertility further dulled Lily's libido, as she viewed herself as broken. As a result, Brenner often felt like he had to beg for her attention, leaving him feeling emasculated and crippling his self-confidence.

"I don't understand what I have to do to make you interested in me," he would lament, rendering Lily frustrated and even less willing to engage in intimacy. Tonight, however, his green eyes seemed to twinkle with passion for life, with hope. She found herself overwhelmed by her desire for him, forgetting the pizza in the oven and more importantly, forgetting the concert tickets. She let him slide her pants off and she took him in.

Brenner felt Lily's soul mingling with his own in a way he hadn't felt in many months, causing him to finish rather sooner than he would have hoped. He was embarrassed and somewhat annoyed. He had tried telling her that the longer they go between having sex, the more abbreviated his stamina would become, and thus the overall quality of sex would reduce. She never wanted to go for another round anymore, like she used to. Moreover, the frequency of expressing his desire for Lily was inversely correlated with her willingness to partake, leaving them in an awkward, frustrated state of dissatisfaction.

Lily recognized Brenner's disappointment with his performance and felt an almost ethereal urge to go again. She took her top off and grabbed his head, pressing it against her bare chest. A look of giddy surprise on Brenner's face strengthened her own desire and they made love again, starting on the couch and finishing on the floor, neither one of them noticing the smell of burning pizza until their panting stopped.

"The pizza!" Lily shouted, as she regained her senses. Brenner watched as she stood up and ran into the kitchen, eyes glued to her rear as it bounced its way towards the oven.

"It's okay, we can just order some," Brenner said as he pulled his underwear back on. "What time do you want to leave tomorrow? The trailhead is about two hours away." Lily didn't answer. Assuming she didn't hear him over the sound of the pizza-shaped charcoal hitting the bottom of the trash can, he asked again.

"Bren," Lily said softly, looking at her husband and then to the ground.

Brenner's heart sank, as he knew this voice. The love of his life was about to strip away the week's remaining happiness, leaving him bare. "You're not going, are you?"

"There's a concert in Charleston, Bren. Carly and Sandra asked me to go with them. Remember, you made me cancel last time to go visit your parents." She began pressing her perceived advantage.

"Fuck it. I'll go alone," he said in defeat. Brenner was tired of fighting and arguing. He remembered when Lily used to ask him to go camping and fishing. Hell, he'd thought she LIKED camping and fishing. Now he wondered if it had just been a trap to catch what she thought would be a suitable husband. He didn't care. He liked spending time with her. He was still hopelessly in love with Lily, and it didn't matter what motivation was behind her wanting to spend time with him. Time was time.

So secure in his loyalty was Lily that she subconsciously let her effort in their relationship slip. Brenner would be there forever, regardless of how she prioritized him. She knew it, and more importantly, he knew it. He was betrayed by his own loyal and hopelessly romantic spirit. Sure, he had fantasies—who didn't? But, never once had he legitimately considered sharing his heart with anyone but Lily. That was the saddest part in his mind. All he wanted was her, and he felt she rarely gave him that.

At least they had a dog.

Of course, Brenner failed to realize that Lily wanted and needed more from her husband than sexual intimacy and adventures. She wanted help with projects around the house and the yard. She couldn't remember the last time Brenner had washed dishes or had done laundry. The only reason Sam continued living was because Lily fed her, not Brenner. Intimacy was not as easy for her as it was for him. It was more the culmination of her appreciation of him as a supportive and helpful husband, qualities that seemed to escape him of late, than it was raw physical desire.

But in this moment, Lily saw just how deeply her words cut the already emotionally exhausted man sitting awkwardly mostly naked on their living room floor. Shame washed over her, making her acutely aware of her exposed body—her breasts, her womanhood. She hurriedly pulled her clothes back on.

The moment of passion, of happiness, vanished as if it had never existed.

What was the point?

She watched as Brenner walked through the kitchen and into the study, where he sat at the Steinway and began playing Chopin's Nocturne in C-sharp Minor, a representation of the loneliness he felt in a marriage he so desperately still wanted.

She used to love his playing, used to be mesmerized by the way his fingers moved over the keys. But now the music felt empty, as pointless as their interlude had been.

She sighed and got up to order delivery.

***

Brenner's night was sleepless as he tossed and turned, his stomach churning beer and pizza grease until it bubbled over, its burning acidity strongly perceived by his lower esophageal sphincter. At around two in the morning, he sighed loudly, almost hoping that Lily would wake and ask him what was wrong. He stood up and staggered through the darkness to the bathroom to pop four antacids. The chalky, minty flavor was forever associated with heartburn, and he resented the taste as he crawled back into bed. He mentally and sarcastically thanked his mom's side of the family for inherited acid reflux.

Brenner looked over at his wife who was still peacefully sleeping and groaned. Why didn't she care about him? How can she sleep so peacefully after their conversation, one that extended far beyond what was described in the kitchen? What could he possibly do better in their marriage?

Being empathetic to a fault and quick to blame himself for everything, he began latching onto every part of himself as a reason for his wife's apparent negligence towards him. For a thirty-two-year-old, his appearance mirrored that of a high schooler, which was admittedly the thing he hated most about himself. It was constantly thrown at him, every time he ordered a beer or bought nicotine.

"I was blessed with a youthful face." "I'm older than I look." "When I'm your age, I won't look so decrepit."

He had about ten of these phrases, ones he repeated over and over—desperate distractions from the deep-seated hatred he felt for his appearance. His collection of self-platitudes was about as limited as his stock of professional consolations. And just as ineffective.

Taking a momentary pause from self-evaluation, Brenner listened to the crickets chirping outside the bedroom window and watched a moon shadow lazily pass through the room. He remembered his mother lying with him in bed as a child when he had nightmares, telling him he could determine the temperature outside by the cadence of chirps. Like counting the seconds between lightning and thunder, it wasn't an exact science.

Life, likewise, was a frustratingly inexact science. Actions caused reactions. Every force was acted upon by an equal and opposite force. Hypotheses were tested and either nullified or accepted. Yet it all seemed rather unpredictable, and he continued trying to figure out which action of his resulted in the reaction of a distant wife. His job, maybe. It's true he hadn't spent much time at home in the last year. Things were supposed to be better after he had finished school, yet he was still home past a reasonable dinner time most nights.

Feeling a half-deserved sense of heavy, oppressive guilt, he leaned over, whispered, "I'm sorry, Lil," and kissed his wife on her soft, moonlit forehead. She stirred, opened her eyes, jumped in alarm, and exclaimed, "What are you doing?"

"Nothing, I'm just being sweet," he said shyly, feeling embarrassed.

Lily looked at her phone to check the time. "Jesus, Bren. It's two thirty in the morning. Go to sleep. We can talk tomorrow." Obviously annoyed, she rolled over and fell back to sleep in less than thirty seconds, leaving Brenner with his thoughts once more, a place he was slowly realizing, whether he liked it or not, felt like home.

Chapter 3

On Saturday morning, Brenner regretfully awoke from a dream he wished to dwell on when Sam jumped on the bed and began licking the sweat off his face. He had always been an active dreamer and usually woke up looking as if he had lived out his dream in the real world, hair disheveled, face sticky, smelling stale; he called it "morning smell". His senses preceded his brain in wakefulness, and he warmly grabbed Sam's head to tell her good morning.

A sense of incompleteness passed over him when he looked over to see Lily picking out her concert outfits. She held up a white crop top blouse and a pair of exceedingly revealing jean shorts and nodded affirmatively, tossing them to the pile of underwear and toiletries on the mattress beside him. He noticed the black thong on the bed and sighed, imagining someone else getting to see her wearing it after drunkenly dancing at the concert that had replaced his camping trip. He longingly remembered their first camping trip together and the intimacy that steamed up the inside of the small green tent. They shared a sleeping bag that night, something she wouldn't dream of subjecting herself to at this stage in their marriage.

Brenner trusted his wife. At least, he thought he did. Moments like this let slender tendrils of doubt weasel their way into his mind. He could almost feel them climbing the back of his neck, creeping into his skull, tickling his subconscious with quiet menace.

What if she did cheat?

Then he would know it wasn't meant to be. A relief? Not exactly. An answer, maybe.

He was lost in a spiral of self-consuming thoughts—shapeless, baseless, undeserving of the mental space they occupied. With a slow exhale, he shook them off, pushing through the lingering haze of sleep.

Without a word to Lily, he trudged past her, down the creaking wooden stairs toward the kitchen—and, more importantly, the coffee pot. His head felt heavy, and as he moved, he scraped the last remnants of sleep from the corners of his eyes.

"You aren't going to talk to me?" Lily asked as she joined him in the kitchen.

"I don't have anything to say."

"Fair enough."

"Lil, I'm exhausted, okay? The only thing that got me through this hellish week at work was the thought of camping with YOU. I don't give a rat's ass about camping alone." This wasn't entirely true, as he often camped alone. But nonetheless, he continued, "I wanted to spend time with you. I missed you this week." Maybe she would reconsider, seeing how much he adored her and longed for her.

"I'm sorry, but I'm really excited to have time with the girls."

"Is that why you packed my favorite thong?" Brenner knew it was a mistake when the words left his mouth, and he wished he could take them back.

"What the hell is that supposed to mean? If I wanted to cheat on you, I already would have. It wouldn't be hard."

"Is that a fact? Well, it wouldn't be hard for me either." Brenner thought of one of his assistants at work who cornered him in the kennel the previous week wanting to show him the new tattoo she'd gotten. On her sternum.

It had taken willpower to decline, knowing she wanted him to see more than just her tattoo.

"Well, maybe you should just do it, Bren. Is that what you want?"

"No, I was just saying—" He felt anger well up. "—Obviously I don't want that. I just don't know—"

"It might be your favorite thong, but it's also my favorite pair of underwear. No one is going to see it except for me, and possible Carly and Sandra."

Brenner thought of Carly and Sandra walking around the room in their underwear, which distracted him from his irrational fear of Lily cheating. "Whatever. I'm going to go unpack your camping gear."

Brenner slammed the carport door on his way out, leaving Lily frustratedly sighing at the coffee pot. She considered bringing him the coffee he'd poured but then forgotten. She also briefly entertained the idea of forgoing the concert to join her husband. She decided against doing either, realizing she had no interest in going with him. He was in such a sour mood, throwing a tantrum like an immature child. Who wanted to spend a weekend with someone like that? And even if he'd be in a better mood if she came, should she be rewarding this kind of behavior?

"Maybe one of these days you will want to spend time with me," he said passively aggressively as he came back into the kitchen and scooped up his now no-doubt lukewarm coffee. She hated the attitude, hated the way he put everything into black and white. Like she couldn't want to spend time with friends and still also want to spend time with him. It was maddening.

"Be safe," she said quietly.

"Yeah, you too."

"Hey, Bren," Lily said as she followed him to his vehicle. "Look at me, I love you."

"I love you, too."

They kissed and then Brenner finished loading up the 4Runner, alone. He watched his wife in the rear-view mirror as he pulled down the driveway. A strange feeling passed over him when she finally looked away and began walking towards the house, a feeling he couldn't quantify, but one that felt heavy and foreboding. Somewhere deep in his subconscious a voice told him to turn around. He physically shook his head, tossing the voice aside. They'd be okay, he told himself, they always had been.

Brenner felt the proverbial wind in his sails as he merged onto the highway and set his compass North, towards the eventual destination of Big Creek Campground near Clyde, North Carolina. The only silver lining he could find in Lily not joining him was that he would be able to fly fish. Lily had no patience for fishing these days and, if he was going to drag her into the woods, he thought it only fair he not abandon her to go fishing himself.

Big Creek was full of colorful, wild rainbow trout. He glanced at the flies he had hooked through the fabric on the ceiling of his truck. Royal Wulff, San Juan Worm, Parachute Adams, Blue Winged Olive, Pheasant Tail, Hares Ear.

The sight of the flies reawakened his frequently suppressed desire to live in the mountains, somewhere he could fly fish whenever he wanted. But fate—rather, the choices he had made, but that would put blame on himself which Brenner couldn't quite stomach—restricted his existence to the land of brothy bass ponds and mosquitos. He hated warm water fishing with such passion that he would rather be at work than dripping with sweat wiping pond scum from his wading boots. At least he was only a few hours from trout streams, though he rarely found time to drive to them.

For most of the drive, the cab was filled with loud music from a playlist titled "Mountain Weekend." When it looped back to the beginning for the third time, Brenner shut off the stereo and rolled down the windows.

Less than an hour from Knoxville, Tennessee, he navigated the winding roads, sweeping curves revealing panoramic vistas of Blue Ridge valleys and ribbon-like streams far below the bridges. The air was crisp and clean. He opened his mouth and took a deep breath, letting it fill his lungs.

***

At around the same time, Lily lowered her windows as she crossed the Ashley River in Charleston, nearing her friend Sandra's house in West Ashley. However, the air she breathed lacked the purity of mountain breezes; instead, it was thick with the almost artificial scent of pluff mud—the final gift marshes bestow on the Earth as vegetation decays. Lily didn't think about it in such scientific terms. To her, it was just an unpleasant smell, and she had little interest in the endless "but why?" questions about nature and biology that cluttered her husband's mind. Be-sides, she was preoccupied with thoughts of the concert. Her favorite hot country artist would soon be sweating and dancing on stage, releasing beautiful music into the low-country air that would easily offset any annoying odors. *Soon*, she thought, look-ing over at the mini bottles—or nips, as Yankees call them—of Fireball cinnamon whiskey.

"Hey, ladies!" Lily announced as she opened the door minutes later to find Sandra and Carly dolled and liquored up, an obvious precursor to responsible decision making.

Always the class act, Carly responded with a, "Hey, you sexy bitch!" and ran to Lily with a half-empty bottle of Tito's vodka. "You look thirsty."

It drove Lily crazy, but she had to admit Brenner might be right when he theorized that the least attractive member of a friend group was generally the vilest in language and action. In college, Carly had had a bad habit of compensating for her lack of male attention by trying to make it as easy as she possibly could for any man who did look her way. To point that out was heartless, Lily would tell Brenner, but privately she admitted it was hard to deny.

"I'm desiccated," Lily said.

"How mad was Brenner?" asked Sandra.

"He's fine. I mean, he'll be fine. He usually forgets about me when he's fishing. I'm not worried."

With forced nonchalance, Lily took a long pull from the translucent, potato-fermented vodka—its flavor leaving a lot to be desired. She used to be able to handle her liquor. She used to be cool, she thought, back in college when she dated whoever she wanted—month by month, week by week, sometimes day by day—without any responsibilities, her whole life and all her dreams still before her.

Free-spirited, they called it. Some, at least.

She was determined to be that girl again tonight. If she was going to disappoint her husband, the night had better be worth it. The opener would play for at least two hours, with an intermission around nightfall before the headliner. Lily hadn't drunk this heavily during the day for several years—the last concert with Sandra and Carly—and thought of the role model she wished to be for her students. Then she thought of her argument with Brenner and the need for distraction.

"Let's get wasted."

***

Brenner, meanwhile, was not any closer to being cool. While his wife was trying to regain, or regress to, the free-spirited, self-absorbed, dare-we-say unique sorority girl she had once been, Brenner was tamely, and utterly uninspiringly, stepping out of his vehicle into what seemed to him like Heaven.

He took a moment to enjoy the warm unpolluted rays that filtered through the canopy, warming his face and the living forest floor. The soft, tendrilled moss on river stones exhaled small motes of moisture that hung in suspension above them, transforming the sunshine into a three-dimensional glow, as if the carpeted green mats radiated their true spiritual selves into the plane of human observation.

He thought of Lily and how inconceivable it was that she'd rather be stuck in West Ashley than here, soaking in the tranquility of Southern Appalachia.

The roaring symphony of the nearby waterfall pleasantly drowned all self-pity thoughts out of his head and Brenner closed his eyes. He imagined each droplet dancing its way downstream, around dulled river stones, under partially submerged oak limbs, and finally pulled by gravity over the stony ledges, cast through the mountain air to the climactic resolution at the foot of the waterfall, before journeying onto to the next fall, until some unknown moment when the Atlantic Ocean would welcome it back to the sea.

Here his soul seemed free, almost reborn, stripped of stressors, all undeserving of the weight he put on them, but greedy with appetite for thoughts and moments of passing time that one can never retrieve. Deep in the valleys of blue Brenner's soul would detach from the captivity of his possessive mind and skirt all around his periphery, interacting with the souls of nature that most people doubt exist. Brenner's cerebrum, and thus his conscience, may not have believed the ecosystem around him was a beautiful spiritual intertangling, but his soul knew it, as it introduced itself to the virgin forest. Somehow, he felt it, without ever consciously articulating it.

***

"I can't wait to find some drunk cowboy-looking guy to dance with tonight," Carly blurted out as she sat in the back seat of Sandra's car and watched a two-masted sailboat dock. They were crossing over the Ashley River back into Charleston proper, the location of the much-anticipated concert. Technically, Carly had a boyfriend. They'd been dating two years now but somehow it was a weekend for revisiting less encumbered times. Lily could understand the impulse.

"Now, now, we can have fun tonight without doing anything we regret. Remember last time?" Sandra looked in the rear-view mirror to cast a reproving, yet amused, glance at Carly, who shrugged and giggled.

"I only regretted it the next morning when I had to call you to come get me. I don't regret what happened."

"On that note," Lily started, "it's time to pass *this* around." She unscrewed the cap from an oversized bottle of that year's grocery store-brand red blend, all qualities that indicated the utmost quality to the seasoned connoisseur.

Mouths hued purple from subsequent sips—gulps—of wine, the ladies arrived at the outdoor venue in North Charleston, a location that would have been far more dangerous just ten years prior. Carly, for some reason, misjudged the distance from the vehicle to the ground and her foot impacted the gravel rather firmly, forcing a diaphragmatic contraction, likely an attempt to gasp. Instead, Carly belched loudly.

"Ew, Carly! What the hell?" Sandra said as Lily started laughing.

"C'mon girls, let's go. We're missing the opener!" Lily dragged them forward, all three walking at a slight angle that would not be corrected until they happened upon the fence—not to be confused with any sort of gate—ten feet right of admissions.

***

Brenner, meanwhile, had set his sights on Midnight Hole, a deep blue plunge pool framed by ancient rock faces covered with creeping rhododendron branches, two miles up a gently climbing trail. The trail was rough, with massive hardwood roots intermixed with trickling mountain water, birthed naturally from the Earth like tears from stone giants. The air was a temperature that brought sweat during climbs and chills on flat, shaded walking. It fluttered through the small, bright green spring leaves, making the mountainside shimmer and sing and filled Brenner's mouth and lungs effortlessly, making intentional breathing seem redundant. He breathed in deep, long drafts of the breeze regardless, savoring its sweet purity, tasting dew-covered bark, saprophytic recycled earth, and the understated hint of wildflower blooms. Overlaying all other appreciable scents was the minerality of mountain water, riding the updraft from the creek to his left.

He disdained people's preference for concerts in planted grass fields on ugly piecemealed stages with artificial light and synthesized sounds. The mountains made their own songs every day. He felt somehow it yearned to be listened to, jealous of mankind's infatuation with human blabbering and artificiality. Each day's song was infinitely different than its temporal predecessor. Wind never winds through trees the same way twice. Water always chooses new paths over river stones. Birds don't chirp their tunes at the same part of the concert. Sadly, Brenner thought, most people aren't quiet long enough to notice. Even when he encountered other hikers, they were often too busy chattering to hear anything above their own noise.

Brenner loved listening to nature sing and nature loved putting all its energy into playing for him the perfect melody, only to replace it with a more beautiful one the next time his feet walked through the valleys.

When he walked down to the hole, the sun parted high clouds and cast uninterrupted sunshine down into the depths of the water, giving the natural vivacity of uncut sapphire. He smiled and again felt the warmth soak into the skin of his face as he started noticing elliptical shapes dart to and fro under the water's surface. A breeze channeled down between the boundary rocks upstream and lifted mist off the surface of the small waterfall, illuminating the immediate area around him in a curtain of ethereal glow. Somewhere above the mountains an eagle screeched.

***

Back in Charleston, the opener was hardly worthy of an open mic night at a college grunge bar, the singer missing notes with a scratchy and painfully achieved falsetto. Better rhythms would be beaten upon drums of any progressive Baptist church in Charleston or Mount Pleasant the next morning. However, the bass guitarist had written "Let's bang" in thick sharpie on the back of his instrument and found every opportunity—some fairly forced—to flip it over in display to the shifting conglomerate of drunken music lovers.

"They are good!" Lily shouted to Carly, as the musician once again projected his desire for sex with random drunk girls, many of whom were likely beyond the point of reasonable consent.

An expert in modern music herself—that is to say, cheaply inspired electronic, instrumentless pop that plagiarizes country songs of days gone by—Carly took her attention away from the "cowboy" rubbing up on her from behind and responded, eloquently, "SO good!" Dizzy headed with evaporated inhibitions, Carly then turned and kissed the average-looking guy with the oversized cowboy hat, the likes of which would get him beat up in a bar in Montana or Wyoming, where real cowboys still exist and suffer not hipster young professional assholes. True love.

"Here we go again," Lily said, nudging Sandra and pointing her attention to their graceful and modest friend locking lips with the sweaty stranger. They rolled their eyes and then pushed through the crowd towards the bar to get another bucket of

Coors Light, hopefully still with blue mountains, not that they would really take the time to notice.

***

Brenner had just released his sixth dainty, energetic rainbow trout back into Midnight Hole, taking time to appreciate the streaks of color God decided to paint across its body long before modern man existed, giving it a vibrancy far exceeding its name, which is manmade. *The name God would have given this beauty*, Brenner thought, *would be in a language surpasses our understanding and hearing it would imprint the spirit of the fish on our souls in such a way as to lend knowledge of its true nature. Instead, we call them rainbow trout and are left still only in partial appreciation and partial understanding.* "It's the task You gave to Adam, but we've done a pretty poor job." When Brenner spoke softly to God, barely audible over the bubbling creek, he could feel his knowledge of the world around him grow ever-so-slightly larger, or perhaps deeper.

Seeing the falling afternoon sun begin to dip behind the rolling horizon, only an hour from mountainous eclipse, Brenner packed his fly rod and took a path he knew intersected with the Appalachian Trail, around two miles from his current position. His goal was to have the tent pitched and dinner steaming by the time total darkness arrived, allowing him to peacefully choose bedtime, rather than toiling in darkness—

which begets anxiety. For the most part though, he no longer feared the wild night but relished the quiet.

Forty minutes later, sitting on a log beside his tent, Brenner rehydrated a bag of Mexican rice with boiling water and added slices of cheap, pungent smoked sausage—a proper camping meal, hearty and restorative for the gut.

He scooped up a first bite, but the moment it hit his tongue, he spat the blisteringly hot, half-melted mass onto the ground, cursing under his breath. He already knew the rest of the meal would be ruined—diminished to a dull, muted version of its original flavor, now layered with the tasteless sting of a burnt tongue. They say "good things come to those who wait". Burnt mouths come to those who take premature bites.

***

Meanwhile, Lily and her friends were losing their voices singing, or rather, shouting beautifully into the humid marshy air that hovered around the music venue, their voices joining the thick fog of spent cigarettes and vape clouds. To their left, a girl knelt above a pile of fresh vomit comprised of a partially digested corn dog in a broth of cheap beer.

Lily and her friends felt for her, but in danger of following suit themselves—they were on their third bucket of beer—they decided to take a walk to the river with their new friends, the cowboy and his buddies, a bearded foul-mouthed redhead and someone trying, and failing, to emulate Patrick Swayze from Point Break. These were hot guys only when viewed with the glossy eyes of inebriation, but it was still a turn on to the women to know they were desirable. They weren't going to *do* anything, but it was a thrill to know they could.

Lily looked back as they approached the dock to make sure they were well within view—and shouting distance—of the crowd. She wanted to have fun, sure, but she didn't want to be completely alone with these strangers.

"Come on, no one is looking," the beard said as he stepped over the small concrete barrier onto the easily overlooked dock that extended like a thorn over the dark, salty waters of the Cooper River. The five-remaining land-bound members of the party looked at each other, shrugged, and followed him onto the wooden planks, doing their best to put one foot in front of the other in a coordinated fashion until they reached the end of the dock which opened into a wider platform meant for docking boats. Dangling shoeless feet into the water, they longingly stared at the moon and the clear stars, vocalizing some manufactured and lofty thoughts into the night air at each other, thinking themselves poetic and inspired, unaware their sentiments were cheap and overexpressed, grasped-at thoughts that were simply higher than their drunken minds' capacity for understanding, but more importantly, they were spoken to impress and not as an expression of true feeling. Nevertheless, these pointless words circled the group for several minutes until Sandra with a satisfied, content smile leaned back and let her body come to rest on the dock.

The bearded philosopher, who had led most of the esoteric, spiritual conversation about heavenly bodies moments before must have felt proud of himself and decided to try his luck. He put his arm around Lily, who took slightly longer than normal to react, and leaned in for a kiss. Lily, for her part, backed away and firmly removed his arm. “I’m married. Please stop.” Carly rolled her eyes at her boring, prude friend, but was reminded that she had a cowboy to kiss, which she began to do in earnest.

Lily was glad when Sandra started talking a few moments later, replacing the noisy make out session that was happening on the other side of her. “You guys heard what happened here last year, right?”

“In Charleston?” Lily responded.

“No, on this dock. It’s actually terrifying!”

Carly stopped kissing the cowboy and they both turned to listen to Sandra.

“Last year a high school kid committed suicide here, right where we’re sitting.”

“Holy shit, Sandra. Why didn’t you tell us that before?” Carly asked, squirming to adjust her position.

"That's not the worst part; the whole story is heartbreaking. The boy's father drowned a few miles upriver from here two months before, but his friends said…"

"Said what?" Lily asked.

"Well, it's weird—I can't believe you didn't hear about this. It was a huge story on the news… Anyway, his friends swore that he believed his dad was alive! He said he'd been talking to him every day since he died."

"Jesus," one of the guys murmured.

"He said he was going to meet his dad by the river the day he shot himself."

"That's horrifying," Lily said after a long silence.

"Yeah, I think I'm ready to go back to the concert. I don't want to be on the dock anymore." Carly stood up and started turning towards the crowd.

The surfer, Patrick Swayze wannabe, desperate for attention since Sandra seemed to possess morals and refused his advances, was unfazed by the story and announced a horrible idea. "Yo guys, what if we jumped in?"

"Are you crazy?" Sandra asked.

Lily for the first time that night thought of Brenner, knowing jumping in the river is precisely the thing he would do if he were there, albeit not drunk, a word which grossly understates her current condition. He refused to let anything scare him. In fact, he would take it as a challenge to jump.

No one said anything for several moments, long enough for everyone but Lily to think the proposition was firmly rejected. One by one, the members of their party began walking towards the ramp. Lily, however, found herself missing her husband and wanted to be like him. She wanted to be carefree and brave. "I'll jump if someone goes with me," she finally said, quietly.

Sandra spun around and responded, "No, Lily, you will not. Don't be stupid."

The surfer, realizing he had a taker and hoping somehow this bonded experience might blossom into a short-lived romantic encounter, ignored Sandra, and turned his attention towards Brenner's wife. "Let's do it! The rest of y'all are chicken shits!" They stood up and shook off the small fear that clung to both of their minds when they stared into the dark, consuming water.

"Don't!" Sandra shouted as Lily started counting.

"...three!"

At that moment, Lily and her new companion leapt from the dry, stable dock into the water.

Despite being a strong swimmer, she was instantly shocked by the force of the outgoing tide as it yanked her away from her friends, dragging her toward open water. Panic seized her, colliding with the sudden realization of just how drunk she truly was.

Her arms and legs thrashed wildly, cutting through the water in frantic, erratic strokes—but they found no purchase. The current pulled her farther and farther away. Her head spun, and as she gasped, a mouthful of water rushed into her throat, cutting off her breath.

"Help!" she choked out, her voice barely breaking the surface.

The surfer, equally drunk but accustomed to the tides and a better swimmer, started to chase her in the current. "Swim to me! Swim this way!" The two other men jumped into the water and followed their friend towards the quickly vanishing girl they had just met. Sandra and Carly screamed from the dock and pointed to where they last saw Lily, the angle of their pointing becoming more obtuse the further from the dock her figure drifted.

Just when Lily thought she was starting to successfully make some ground back towards the dock she felt something grab her leg. A hand. She tried to scream but was pulled below the surface before any noise escaped. Her voice was replaced by soundless, large bubbles.

By the time the surfer reached where he thought she was, Lily was nowhere to be found. No splashing. No screaming. No wake. Just a quiet, disrespected full moon Atlantic tide, echoing subtle eerie splashes off the structure of the dock behind him.

***

Brenner had no trouble falling asleep to the sounds of the mountain evening, far from the problems that kept his tired mind wakeful at home. His head lay comfortably on the down jacket he'd worn that morning, and his body was tightly hugged by his sleeping bag. He exhaled toxins with each unconscious sleeping breath and replaced them with purity of the spirit that can only be found somewhere far, far from the rest of the world. However, he was awoken by a disturbance in the night.

He felt something, or at least he thought he did. His eyes opened quickly as his mind tried to process whether what woke him was in his dream or in his tent. He was surprised to see light outside, bright light. Thinking it was morning, he tried to sit up but found himself unable to move. The air was suddenly cold and bitter, and he became aware of a deep rumbling sound that seemed unearthly and vibrated through his body like the ground itself was moaning. His heart started racing and he felt it skip every third beat. The moaning grew louder and deeper as it reverberated in his mind causing pressure to build in his skull. He started screaming in panicked, painful delirium, still unable to move.

Then the scratching started. A single nail ran its way up the side of the tent on his left and he could see a line moving. One nail turned to two, then two to three, and then there were nails all around the tent rhythmically pressing into the fabric, climbing up the walls.

The light grew brighter until it seemed the source was inside the tent with him.

Then—silence.

The moaning ceased. The scratching stopped. Only the light remained, flooding the space in an unbearable glow. For ten agonizing minutes, it lingered. At times, Brenner could swear he felt something—something unseen—gliding along his arms, his legs, his chest. The brightness grew, blinding, unbearable. Then came the scream—a piercing, unnatural shriek that tore through the valley, rattling through his skull.

Finally, all at once, darkness swallowed the tent. His breath came in ragged gasps as he lay paralyzed, alone. When he finally gathered the courage to glance at his watch, the glowing numbers read 11:00 p.m.

Chapter 4

Almost two months to the day after Lily's drowning, Brenner stared cross-eyed at a dog's blood chemistry results, eyes trying to pick out individual values before they jumbled together into a mind soup. It had been the ring. The previous client, whose dog's blood work Brenner was attempting to read, was a middle-aged woman, not particularly memorable apart from the diamond engagement ring on her left hand, not an uncommon accessory in that demographic. It was, however, the first ring Brenner had seen that morning.

He had only recently started working again after his wife's death, and every time he noticed evidence of marriage on a woman's finger it sent him spiraling. This time was bad enough he'd overlooked all the swollen lymph nodes on his patient, instead opting for running unremarkable blood work, which he currently struggled to interpret. Fortunately, during the appointment the client became aware of Dr. Miles's seemingly detached state of mind and would take her dog to another veterinarian for a second opinion the next week—lymphoma. Brenner was heartbroken when he eventually found this out.

That morning, as had become his routine, Brenner added a new journal entry about Lilith. His journaling was an attempt to find some sort of closure, something he desperately needed but entirely lacked. He had written about his first interaction with Lily, an event that was difficult to disassociate with his job, since that was where it had taken place:

She came to the appointment with her father, replacing her mom who was busy that morning. Thank God, as her dad knew nothing about Bentley, their lab. Typical husband. I noticed her bare ring finger as she held the dog still for my exam. Though I pretended to listen closely to the history she gave me, my mind was preoccupied with sparks of attraction. I watched her mouth move as she explained Bentley's propensity for coprophagia—eating shit. Not normally a sexy topic but the way her lips were tenderly flexing, opening, closing, as her tongue contorted, pressing against different parts of her mouth to make beautiful sounds. As I began offering solutions to her father's dog's issues, her green-speckled hazelnut gaze rested on my mouth. She gave an answering grin. Did she hear what I was saying? It didn't matter. Her dad was unaware that despite talking about Bentley, his daughter and the vet were playing an unspoken game. A pretended accident, her hand touched mine under Bentley's chest. I ran a finger across her soft palm as I reached for my stethoscope.

The appointment ended without an opportunity for me to ask for her name, much less her phone number. I cursed myself for the remainder of the day, as butterflies bounced around in my stomach. I was on call that night and groaned when my phone started ringing five minutes before the shift ended, our call service telling me Bentley's "sister" was calling to check in. "Hey, it's Lily. You saw my dad's dog today. I know calling like this is kind of nuts, but I was hoping I'd catch you. I was wondering if you wanted to grab coffee some time?"

It might have helped to focus on when things had started to sour, but that's not how the human mind works. Death has a way of wiping the slate clean, so that one tends to remember only those memories that fill a heart with love and longing, a perfected version of the bygone relationship, warts and wrinkles removed.

Gone were the arguments, the lack of intimacy, the not-so-rare fear Lily wouldn't love him forever, and even the fear she would cheat on him. He remembered his wife pure as the driven snow, a collection of every quality befitting the embodiment of a flawless companion, one that seemed destined to be his as long as the world—or at least the capacity for love and affection—had existed. He remembered her as the version of Lily he flirted wordlessly with in the exam room over Bentley's head.

Brenner closed his eyes and lost a little more of his motivation to work up the sick patient that currently sat in the very same exam room as the passage in his journal had taken place. It started as a shudder that he felt most acutely in his jaw as he breathed in deeply. When he opened his eyes, his vision was blurred, and his eyelids trembled. *Not again*, he thought, as he tried to blink away the wetness. He rose from the computer and started walking towards the small bathroom, hiding his face from the rest of the office staff. The bathroom was locked, likely occupied by a client. *Damn it.*

He quickly walked through the treatment area and continued down the hallway towards the back door of the clinic, anywhere away from onlookers. His emotions were not well hidden as he passed Emily, who started to say something but was restrained by a cautionary head shake and stern look from Dr. Johnson. He heard a quiet conversation, with him as the subject, begin as he exited the building and shut the door behind him. He had become accustomed to having emotional breakdowns in front of the staff and it became less and less embarrassing, his self-respect all but evaporated in the glaring reality of his loss. He collapsed on the bed of pine straw that butted up to the back wall of the clinic and allowed himself to melt fully, leaving tear tracks down his cheeks. An episode of dry heaving led to vomiting onto the straw, immediately before Ben walked out of the back door to sit next to him.

"Bren, you can't keep going on like this. I get it, you want to work. But this isn't good for you. You have to heal." Dr.

Johnson put his arm around Brenner and looked at him with sincere compassion and empathy.

Brenner cleared his nose forcefully in preparation for talking. "It's not good for my patients. I can barely concentrate. I'm sorry."

"I'm not worried about the patients. I'm worried about you."

"I don't know if…" Brenner looked down at the ground and let the silence linger for a moment as he thought about his words. "…if I'm ready to be back."

"Listen, you know you have a place here for as long as you want. Take some more time, Brenner. Go heal. Go have an adventure and don't worry about us. We'll hold the fort down and be here when you're ready."

Chapter 5

There are more than 300 miles of the Appalachian Trail stretching through North Carolina, from where it enters the state in the south, from Georgia, up to where it exits into the rolling, green mountains of Virginia via Tennessee's northeastern corner.

Brenner's heart had always been drawn—by nature, God, or some combination of the two—to the misty blue ridges of the Smoky Mountains. He had long fixated on the idea of hiking the entire section of the Appalachian Trail that ran through them.

The problem had been time—there was never enough of it.

Brenner had often found himself envious of the adventuresome—though financially unstable—friend of the aforementioned assistant Stephen, whose name was Jeff. This twenty-three-year-old, frequently unemployed member of society had been gifted a sleeper van by his parents, whose ambitions for their offspring had always outpaced his own.

Jeff used his free time—all his time was free—to drive out west and see the country, one state at a time. *It must be nice,* Brenner would think to himself as Stephen shared picture after picture.

So, when Dr. Johnson suggested Brenner take some time to heal, the wheels started spinning and he chose his adventure. He would hike from Georgia to Virginia along the Appalachian Trail with Sam. The mountains had always healed him before, and he trusted they wouldn't fail this time. Of all places he could take his battered heart, the ridges and valleys of smoky blue, full of life and hope, and more importantly, a natural world that continues living indefinitely outside the realm of all of our problems and heartbreak seemed the most likely place to find himself again, to find the part of Brenner that might still be living somewhere out in the wilderness, somewhere safe.

***

It was the evening of July 4 when Brenner started packing, accompanied in his workshop by his best-remaining friend and strongest living connection to Lily, Sam, the almost three-year-old coonhound, who nervously paced back and forth with the reports of celebratory trinitrotoluene echoing in the background, flashing bright, multicolored light through the dirty, cobweb-ridden window, repeated shadows cast around the dimly lit room.

"Fucking fireworks," Brenner mumbled as he reached towards his dog. "Come here girl, it's okay." Sam looked up at him with soft, brown trusting eyes as to say, "I believe you, but I'm still scared." *I don't envy being at the clinic tomorrow,* he thought. He pictured the appointment bin full of "diarrhea that started last night" histories. Brenner had liked fireworks as a child, but his time in veterinary medicine gave him a deep loathing for America's brash way of celebrating freedom. He felt bad for all the dogs and horses who either thought they were being shot at, were stuck amid a bad thunderstorm, or some combination of the two.

A particularly bright red flash, probably from the neighbors' display, illuminated the bottom right shelf against the back wall of the shop. Brenner choked as it brought his attention to the forlorn pile of Lilly's camping gear. The pink backpack, orange sleeping bag, relatively new camping hammock, a deck of "America's National Parks" themed playing cards… Lilly had loved playing games. As soon as they got into their tent for the night, she would always immediately start dealing out cards. Brenner pretended to hate playing so often, but he was hopelessly in love with Lilly and her spirit for games—perhaps just her levity—made his heart twist into passionate knots and his stomach fill with butterflies. He always lost, but mostly because he couldn't keep his eyes and hands off the dealer.

The camping mug he was holding gently slid out of his nerveless left hand and bounced to the floor as he continued to focus on each one of his wife's possessions sitting lonely and now forever unused on the shelf, like relics of an age past. He followed the mug down as he too slid to the ground and his hands braced his weight, open on the cold concrete floor. Eyes watering, he felt his abdomen clench. As tears flowed from his eyes and eventually completed their course to wet the concrete, he began the recently familiar act of dry heaving. He cursed the world, and he cursed God for what He had let happen to him until he had no more energy to produce sound. He surrendered to the fetal position on the floor listening to the dwindling distant explosions until at last he was left in the night alone, in a room devoid of sound and light. Another happy Independence Day, come and gone.

The dog sat and watched with a partially confused understanding. Finally, she let out a soft whine and came to nudge Brenner. He rolled over so he could see her face, hanging over his with goofy, flopping ears touching his cheeks. She began to lick him, to cheer him up and to taste the salt of his tears. He started laughing and grabbed Sam's head. "God, I love you. You're such a good dog and I'd be so lost without you."

He went on like this for several days, the beginning of his trip consistently pushed back due to his inability to pack for more than twenty minutes in the same room as Lily's memories. He couldn't bring himself to touch or move any of it. In a strange way, he wanted to hurt. He would bring a bottle of whiskey to help with packing and let himself cry, night after night for almost a week before all his gear was ready to go.

The night before embarking on his journey, a Friday, Brenner went to Ben Johnson's house to shoot pool, at the unsurprisingly late hour the latter veterinarian finally made it home from the office. Ben returned from saying goodnight to his wife and kids and poured two fingers of Kentucky straight bourbon into a small glass of ice, handing it to Brenner. "You could use it, kid." If anyone else had referred to Brenner as a kid, it might have elicited a defensive outburst, but Ben loved Brenner, and Brenner looked up to him as a friend, even a mentor. At twenty years his senior, he'd earned the right to "kid" him.

"I don't know what I could use, but this'll be a good start. How are things at work?"

"We miss you," Johnson replied, as he poured his own drink. "The staff and the clients miss you, but we wouldn't want you there at the expense of your own wellbeing. Are you all set for leaving tomorrow?" He finished racking the balls and nodded at Brenner to break.

"I think so…" Brenner whispered as he sent the cue ball down the table. *Smack.* The seven-ball glided into the corner pocket.

"I guess you're solids." Ben took a sip of whiskey. "How are you holding up?"

Holding up… There was no holding up. Holding up would imply there was something left to be held up, that his life had structure, substance, and organization. No such things any longer existed. There was only moving forward with the hope and the prayer that forward would bring a dulling to the pain.

"I'm holding up alright, I guess," he lied, as he pretended to give a shit about pool. The two-ball sat nervously by the side pocket, as if it wanted to be pocketed, to disappear from the plane of visibility, something Brenner related with, as he too longed to vanish from sight and be forgotten. He missed.

"You're not allowed to let me win," Ben said as he studied his young colleague and friend, who usually showcased the skills developed from late nights spent in smoky college town pool halls. Ben frowned as he considered the torrent of emotions compounding the perceived weight of gravity on Brenner's body, nearly immobilizing him. He knew he would heal but hoped for Brenner's sake it would somehow come faster than he knew possible after losing a spouse.

"I don't know how to let someone win. I just suck tonight," Brenner responded. "You know," he looked down at his feet, "I wish life would let *me* win, just once."

"It was a horrible accident, Brenner. You will never

understand why it happened, but it's not for you to understand. Trying to understand it will strip any future happiness. You know my dad died when I was in high school. I spent years ignoring any potential for happiness because I cursed the very nature of the world. I cursed God, I cursed my friends, and I cursed myself. Where did that get me? It certainly didn't bring my dad back. Life can also be beautiful, Brenner, if you let yourself just forgive it and spend your effort chasing the good things."

"The good things?" Brenner snorted and rolled his eyes.

"I know it's not time for you to heal yet, Bren, but please promise me you can see the potential to heal, at least—good shot, by the way."

"I guess we'll find out soon enough." Brenner looked out the window into the dark of night, letting his eyes imagine rocky ridges draped with the pastel blended pink of a morning sunrise or a soft sweeping grassy knoll, touching the thin air of autumn, blades of grass gently fluttering like an ocean in the breeze.

Several hours later, Brenner was sitting in bed with his journal, pen shaking in his hand as he thought of words to write.

Lilith,

The world you left me with is devoid of color, smell, and taste. Three years ago, when I said "I do", I meant it forever. I just didn't know forever was such a short amount of time. I have relived our best memories in my dreams every night. I love being with you, but the pain of having to realize you are gone every time I wake up makes me wish I would never dream again. My thoughts have been darkened to the point that I don't know if I'm coming back from this trip. I am taking life a single, cruel day at a time. I no longer feel that I have any purpose. The only thing left from a life I thought I knew is Sam. I wouldn't be able to continue getting out of bed every morning if it weren't for her.

Why did you do it? Why the hell would you go drunk night swimming in the Cooper? You can't make decisions like that. It doesn't just affect you. You have moved on to a better place now and don't have to deal with the fallout. You've left me alone, broken, and wishing I could have drowned with you. The love in my heart for you is somehow coexisting with a newfound hatred. Not a hatred for you as a person, but a hatred for you leaving me. A hatred for letting myself rely on a single person for so much of my happiness. I would hurt less if I never loved you the way I did—the way I do. I have never hated anything or anyone but now I find myself hating more things than I love. I know a part of me is hiding somewhere in the woods. If I find it, maybe I will heal. If I don't find it, then I'm not sure I can come back. I fear I am too far gone.

-Bren

Chapter 6

Brenner put the haunting loneliness of his and Lily's house in the rearview mirror at around five on the morning of July 10 and started driving towards the quaint mountain town of Clayton, Georgia, and ultimately Dick's Creek Campground. He would have a strenuous nine-mile hike from the parking lot up to the Appalachian Trail at Bly Gap, the starting point for his journey. With each mile he drove west, he felt a small bit of hope and excitement well up in his heart, albeit less than he would have felt a few months prior. Nonetheless, he thought it was a good sign.

He drove through a light misting rain most of the way to Clayton. As he was pulling into the awakening mountain town, already slightly abustle with tourists hoping to hike around Tallulah Gorge, solicit a whitewater rafting guide, or simply shop for lackluster trinkets in the downtown shops, the low clouds began to part and several isolated rays of sunshine began finding their way through the blanket of grey, mixing with the fog to form sheets of layered gleam along the sloping mountainsides.

"We just have to make one stop," he said, as he looked back to the stretching hound in the backseat, who awoke at the transition from smooth, homogenous interstate pavement to winding and undermaintained mountain highways. She looked out the passenger-side backseat window and her eyes widened, apparently in surprise at their new location. Her tail began to wag. "We are going to go for a long *walk*," he said, putting added emphasis on the last word, arguably his dog's favorite word. She started trying to climb into the front seat. "No ma'am, it's not safe in the front seat. The last thing I need right now is for something to happen to you. Besides, why are you so excited? We are stopping to get you a backpack; I'm not carrying your shit too, you know…" Her tail continued to wag.

The elderly store clerk stood behind the counter barely acknowledging the black guy checking out in front of Brenner at the outdoors store. The customer looked to be about Brenner's age and was buying a couple different types of dehydrated meals, obviously embarking on a camping trip himself.

"Here you go," he said as he handed the clerk two wrinkled $20 bills. "I'm headed up to Bly Gap. Getting ready to hike through North Carolina on the trail." Brenner's ears perked up as he recognized his own plans coming from the mouth of the man standing in front of him. The clerk said nothing and ignored the money sitting on the counter. "Do you have any advice for me? Have you hiked up there before?" Still no response.

"He asked you a question," Brenner said, coming to his defense.

The elderly man grumbled, shot Brenner a curious look and said, "Next."

"Wonder who put the stick up this guy's ass," Brenner said over his shoulder as he put Sam's new backpack up on the counter. "I'm hiking the North Carolina AT starting at Bly Gap too. Maybe I'll see you up there!"

"Hell yeah, I'll keep an eye out for you. I haven't been hiking alone before, so if you find me dead somewhere up there, please just make it sound like a cool story for my mom."

Brenner laughed. "Will do, brother. And likewise! Catch you on the trail."

After Brenner paid the unnecessarily grumpy clerk for Sam's backpack, he turned and let out a long, symbolic sigh. He was finally ready to start walking in the woods. No more obstacles stood in the way of the search for his missing soul. While still standing just away from the counter, Brenner closed his eyes and felt them quaver, embracing a moment of indiscernible emotion as a small sliver of hope stirred. As he walked through the doorway back towards his car, he paused to hold it open for a girl about his age, realizing how beautiful she was when she smiled at him. Brenner was somewhat disarmed and even startled by her appearance and hardly realized when his car keys slid from his left hand and landed loudly on the sidewalk. He blushed and fumbled with his words, "Uh, oops," he mumbled as he started to reach for them.

"I got 'em," the girl said, as she leaned down right in front of him. She didn't break eye contact with Brenner as she stood back up and placed the keys in his hands, allowing hers to awkwardly touch his for a moment.

"Oh, thanks." He stared. Her gaze had a depth that made him feel like she could tell stories without uttering a word. Her eyes were a rich three-dimensional brown, shades gradually changing the further you went towards the white and the deeper you peered into the space where her heart might live. He felt somewhat trapped in the present moment, not wishing to leave, suspended, unable to move, say, or do anything. She lingered as well and seemed in no hurry to walk into the store.

"Hope," she said, not much louder than a whisper.

"I—what?" Brenner asked, confused, and worried he misunderstood some simple word. As it turns out, he did not misunderstand the word, but the context.

"My name," she smiled.

"Your name…" Brenner tried to laugh it off. She raised her eyebrows. "Oh, sorry. My name is Brenner!"

"Brenner, that's a cool name. Do you know what it means?" she asked.

"Actually, I don't. I've never really thought about it meaning something."

"You should look it up one day! Anyway, it was nice to meet you, Brenner." With that, Hope vanished from Brenner's life as quickly as she walked into it. With a shake of his head, Brenner pulled himself from the moment, walking to his truck and the current love of his life, Samantha.

"Look what I got you!" Brenner opened the door and was greeted by an exuberantly wagging Bluetick Coonhound, slobber dripping from her mouth as she leaned into the front seat to lick him. "This is so Dad doesn't have to carry all your breakfast…" Wags. "…and lunch…" More wags. "…and dinner!" The most wags. "You goofy thing." He smiled at his dog and realized that, like the girl from the store, Sam could tell stories without saying anything too. She always had and he'd always listened.

After settling into the driver's seat, he sighed again, letting go of the last few months. He rolled the windows down and replaced the emotionally charged breath with one pure and untainted, tasting all the ingredients of the mountain morning.

He paused and appreciated the undefinable nature of this smell, one that was natural and vegetative, with hints of earthy soil and riparian plant matter, maybe even the scent of freshly cut grass, and the dew that rested on tips of leaves. No matter how hard he tried, he couldn't pick out the individual authors of the mosaic fragrance, like a newly rich man feigning the skill to identify individual flavors in cigars or whisky; Brenner liked cigars, whisky, and the mountain air, yet he didn't need to dissect them to appreciate them for their collective natures—simply good.

The new breath that filled Brenner's lungs with a long, deliberate contraction of his diaphragm diffused into his soul and cast over him a feeling of calm and of home, as though this moment existed as a singularity and the events that brought him here had been left behind, the last leg of preparation. He was ready, and a deep peace embraced him when he put the vehicle in reverse to back out onto the highway. *Finally, my heart can rest and heal.*

"Shit!" Brenner yelled as a red pickup blared its horn and swerved into the other lane to avoid hitting his seemingly oblivious 4Runner. He watched as a bearded and maned man with scraggly arms and a confederate flag stamped on his hat leaned almost entirely out of the window to shoot Brenner the most aggressive bird he'd ever seen, making him feel like the man was in his own vehicle, shoving his dirty, cigarette-smelling middle finger in his face. Brenner's heart was pounding vigorously, and he felt an instant cold sweat on his forehead. "Okay," he said to himself in a muffled pant, "Let's wait until we get on the trail to start healing. For now, let's keep our eyes on the road." Sam stared at him with huge almond eyes and ears pressed back to her neck in alarm.

Several minutes later, Brenner was crossing a bridge over the Tallulah which was bidding the last fingers of mist farewell as they—as on every other day—allowed the warmth of the sun to break apart their substance and send them back into the ether to one day become rain or river water once again. The vehicle pushed through an especially dense section of fog and left a wispy hole behind it, edges twisting and twirling as they danced with the draft. A few miles away, a gravel road switched back and forth in a dense Appalachian forest before ending at a rather underwhelming trailhead. Dick's Creek. A few dusty, unmolested cars were scattered around the modest parking lot.

"Nine miles, Sam. Nine uphill miles. That's our goal for the day. I promise we'll take it slow." Brenner leaned over to tighten the straps on his hound's backpack before sliding his own on and doing the same. He wiped a large bead of sweat from his forehead and did the final check of his vehicle. Locked and empty. "Alright, girl. Let's go camping." Samantha's ears perked up and she went bounding across the parking lot and through the opening in the forest marking the trailhead. He counted six other cars in the parking lot including two Subaru Outbacks, one Tacoma, a Dodge Challenger, a minivan, and a Jeep. He rolled his eyes at the stick figure family hiking along the rear window of the minivan and nodded in affirmation when he saw the Tacoma's "Trout Unlimited" license plate. There were also two "Coexist" decals in the parking lot and one could easily venture a guess which vehicles they adorned.

A repetitive, metallic clink acutely found itself front and center in Brenner's mind after ten feet on the trail. "We're not listening to that for hundreds of miles," he said as he struggled to twist around to adjust his mug from hanging off the right side of his pack, where it knocked against the aluminum fly rod tube.

Once the mug was relocated, only the soft sound of rubbing canvas straps and nylon backpack shell mixed with the soft thuds of boot meeting trail. Occasionally, the sound of paws on foliage and dirt was audible as Sam completed large circles, running from Brenner to the very limit of line of sight before turning back around and sprinting back to her owner, as if to ask, "Why are you going so slow?". *She's going to sleep well tonight*, Brenner thought. As his eyes focused on the forest ahead, he noticed a lone southern red oak sitting proudly amidst a stand of shortleaf pines. He thought it kind for the pines to permit the oak to live there, knowing trees have their own means of segregation, releasing pheromones into the ground to distance themselves from the outsiders. Maybe the pines admired the oak as well. Maybe they thought it could teach them something.

He watched as the forest warmed up around him. The air seemed heaviest near the ground, and he could see a shimmer above the dark soil of the trail, where the sun found its warmth most accepted. It didn't take long for Brenner to shed his hiking shirt, letting the backpack ride directly on his warm, damp skin. He'd rather blister than suffer the heat, or so he thought. The beginning of the trail followed a small tributary of Dick's creek, layering a delicate bubbling over the sound of their hiking. Although knowing he needed to reach the Appalachian Trail by nightfall, Brenner had still checked three times to see if the tributary was big enough to hold trout. Probably to his benefit, it was not, and he continued trudging upward.

They reached the first of several sequential knobs at around lunch time. Brenner found a lichen-covered boulder several feet off the trail in a sea of grass and called his dog over. They had gained decent elevation since they started, and he could look down at the shrinking hills in the direction of the trailhead. He admired the topography while opening a pouch of beef jerky, an action that immediately interested Sam. She nuzzled her snout up under his arm and stared at him with desperate longing, gently wagging her tail. He pinched off a small piece of jerky and made her sit before he gave it to her. "It would last longer if you chewed it," he said as she swallowed it whole and continued staring at him like he hadn't given her anything yet. "We have to ration." She sighed.

A breeze swirled the grass around them and pushed its way up the mountainside. Brenner stood and, caving under the weight of his best friend's gaze, tossed a larger piece of jerky up the trail, sending the hound into frenzied pursuit. Not seeing exactly where it landed, his dog relied on her greatest gift—her nose—the product of thousands of years of canid evolution and several hundred more of selective breeding. The white flag of her tail stood erect as she wound careful patterns in the grass near the last known location of the teriyaki-flavored morsel from Heaven. Within seconds, the jerky had been found and, once again, swallowed whole.

"I wish I had your motor," the young vet gasped to his dog several hours later, as he was sweating and heaving after a steep incline and the hound continuing to run circles around him, albeit with less energy and more panting than at the trailhead. A sudden cold breeze pulled Brenner's attention to the horizon. A previous succession of faded green ridges, edges mottled by swaths of foliage, had been replaced by a forward moving cloud, linearly stretching across the junction of mountain and sky, advancing in a deliberate roll from the west. The longer Brenner stared at the cloud, the more he recognized evidence of turbulence in the speed at which it closed the blue space between himself and the front and in the wispy edges that twirled at the cloud's periphery.

Damn, Brenner thought as he began to anticipate a strong summer thunderstorm. The coolness of the breeze pushed leaves around him skyward and revealed their lighter green undersides, giving the mountainsides a shimmer. He quickly pulled his shirt back over his sweating torso and unrolled his raincoat. "Let's go, girl!" Sam picked her nose up from a scent behind him on the trail and pressed forward ahead of Brenner.

The first crack of lightning occurred as the cloud was almost above them, the accompanying thunder echoing through the valleys around him and bouncing off any exposed rock faces, giving it an acoustic depth unlike thunder in the flat land. Brenner shuddered at the fullness of nature's anger, before having the thought that nature persists in an emotionless state, only attributed with emotional sentience by mankind, who exists in the world entirely defined by emotion.

Brenner and Sam picked up their pace and were just shy of jogging as they futilely tried to outrun the storm and make for fewer inevitable steps through the rain that was surely coming. Possibly on cue, a crescendo of static white noise fell out of the sky to his left and grew louder until it began to drown out all the other noises of the trail. He looked and frowned as curtains of rain blotted out the ridge immediately to the west and began climbing up the mountain on which the trail coursed. He pulled his hood over his head and soon was enveloped by a torrential downpour.

The saturated Appalachian forest floor had reached its holding capacity for moisture from previous storms that week and soon the trail turned into a river. Water ran up the sides of his boots and poured into his socks. He cursed as walking pushed water out of the way of his feet, leaving a shallow wake on the trail behind him, and began to look for somewhere to wait out the rain. Sam had ceased her endless circles and clung to his side, nervously looking at him at each illuminating flash of lightning. Brenner thought he could hear her whining occasionally above the all-encompassing sound of the rain.

Fifteen minutes after the rain started, Brenner finally located an overhanging rock several paces into the woods on his right, large enough to keep one person and a dog out of the rain. The angle of the ground underneath was such that water was pulled away and down the mountain, leaving a relatively dry spot to weather out the storm. Once seated out of the rain, Brenner pulled off his raincoat and found a ledge on which to drape his shirt, hoping it would somehow dry in the unknown amount of time it would take for the thunderhead to pass them by. No sooner than he took his shirt off did Sam shake her body and sling water and wet dog smell all over him. Brenner laughed and nudged his dog's shoulder. "Punk."

He sighed and discovered a small string of frustration weaseling its way into his subconscious. Of everything he had in his life to pity over, sitting in the rain in the mountains simply wasn't worthy and he shook his head to cast the thoughts aside. *I could be at work right now.* He smiled while pulling an aluminum flask with his initials stamped on the side out of the front pocket of his backpack. The fragrant whiskey within helped him further shift his attitude from self-pity to admiration of his surroundings as he tasted the sweet burn trickling down the back of his throat. Sometime over the next hour of resting, Sam became conditioned to the storm and allowed herself to sink to the ground and rest her head between her soaked, muddy paws. Brenner watched as her breathing slowed and her chest took longer and longer to fill with each breath. Soon, she began snoring. The peaceful tiredness must have been contagious because several minutes later, Brenner found himself leaning back against a rock and his eyes closed. *Just for a few minutes*, he thought as he drifted out of the world of wakefulness.

"Two in the morning," Brenner sighed to himself when he awoke to the sound of an owl in the distance and checked his watch. "Hey girl, I think we are staying here tonight." Sam stirred and rose to her feet, tail gently wagging at the sound of her person's voice, and likely at the anticipation of a very late dinner. The rain had stopped and the forest around the two of them seemed full of life. Brenner now counted three separate owls hooting into the night, making each other aware of the two travelers hiding under the rocky ledge. Bats chirped and squeaked, flying low above the trees, searching for moths. The moon cast lunar shadows in the shapes of giant trees to the ground around where they sat. Knowing there would be no dry wood for a fire, Brenner started boiling water on his camping stove for dinner and used the soft orange ambient glow to begin unpacking and setting up his tent in a clearing a few paces from the rock.

After feeding himself and his dog, he undressed and crawled into the tent, slowly making his way into the sleeping bag. Sam lay at his feet ready to digest her supper in a peaceful sleep, where she probably hoped to dream of chasing rabbits or playing with puppies, two of her favorite pastimes. Brenner found himself wide awake, having slept most of the afternoon, and pulled out his journal and a black ink pen, which were both tucked away in a waterproof pocket.

Lily,

How does one forget a love like ours? How does one move on from it… I feel like you were as much a part of me as I am a part of myself, so much so that I'm struggling to understand myself in the absence of you. I allowed my soul to become tethered to yours so deeply that I fear what's left isn't viable by itself. Losing you has shattered me. I am currently sleeping somewhere near the Appalachian Trail in Georgia. I'm planning on hiking the entire section through North Carolina in search of myself. If you're somewhere out here, make yourself known to me. Show yourself to me, so that we can have just a small amount of fleeting time together yet again. There is so much I never told you, so many things we never got to do. Had I known our time would be cut so desperately short, I would have pursued you with more of myself every single day I knew you, so that as you make your way to whatever is on the other side of death, no matter what you thought you knew of this world, you would know one thing with complete certainty—how much I love you. I hope you know that. I hope somehow, even as it was all happening, you knew deep down how I feel about you, how I've always felt about you. I wish I could bring you back.

-Bren

Chapter 7

Brenner awoke from a short, mostly restless sleep at around nine in the morning, when Sam whimpered and licked his face, in attempt to express her hunger to the man she assumed forgot to feed her breakfast. He looked at his watch and groaned at the late hour, as well as the steam that built up on the inside of his tent, the summer sun transforming what was once a cool Appalachian evening into something like a sauna. The rain-soaked clothes—and more importantly, Bluetick Coonhound—had provided the small tent with enough evaporation to cause Brenner to gasp for air as he reached for the zipper to let a mid-morning breeze whisk away the humid hell in which he awoke.

He let himself feel the frustration this time as streaks of sweat dripped down his already grimy face. After attempting to wipe away the moisture with a wet sleeve, he simply gave up and accepted the notion that it would be a moist morning pack-up. A quick granola bar and a handful of trail mix would suffice since he was already a day behind schedule. In fact, Sam's breakfast took as long as his did to prepare, and that merely involved pouring some kibble into a bowl. A trickle turned into sheets of salty water cascading down his neck and back by the time he finally cinched his backpack closed, with everything neatly tucked inside. The surrounding forest also seemed to exhale steam as the trees slowly shed the last of the rainwater from the late evening.

"It's going to be toasty, girl," Brenner said to the dog as he took the first forward step of the day. If she was bothered by the heat, she didn't show it, once again sprinting forward with the energy of an unbroken thoroughbred. He chuckled and let her optimism carry them both forward. Once he was in North Carolina, there would be less incline, as most of the AT followed ridges and knobs… or so he thought.

An hour of strenuous, uphill, muddy single track later, Brenner finally crested over the top of an especially steep ridge, gulping in large breaths of wet, warm summer air. He knelt and lifted his dog's face towards his and stared lovingly into her eyes, ignoring his surroundings so much so that he yelled, "Jesus CHRIST!" when he felt the hand on his shoulder. He leaned so far to the left that his backpack accepted a freely given assist from gravity to pull him completely onto his left side, the position from which he looked up at the unshaven face and unwashed hair of the sandal-wearing assumed hippie that now offered him a dirty grip with which to pull him back to his feet.

"Sorry about that, brother," the man said in a slow, deliberate voice, as if each word was waiting for the one preceding it to fully vanish before joining in the apology. He stood there and smiled at Brenner, who was still gasping and looking up dumbfounded at the first person—an interesting one at that—he had seen since starting on the trail the morning prior.

"It's, uh, okay, I guess. You scared the living shit out of me, man."

"I thought you saw me, dude."

"No kidding." Brenner accepted the offered hand and let the grungy man struggle with much effort and an overwhelming amount of grunting to pull him to his feet.

"The name's Sticks."

"No, it's not." The words came out of Brenner's mouth with no forethought, but rather a mere reaction to the ever-increasingly odd situation he found himself in. *Am I dreaming? Where the hell am I?*

"Yes, it is." The man stared with honest surprise at Brenner's response.

"You mean to tell me your mom and dad, as they held you in the hospital, still wet behind the ears, looked at the doctor and said, 'His name… is Sticks.'"

"Oh no, dude, that would be so bizarre."

"Indeed. So, that begs the question, what is your name?" Brenner was back to his feet now, brushing his pants off, still suspicious he was sleeping, although becoming more convinced he was awake due to the fact his leg hurt from hitting a rock when he fell.

"Sticks—"

"—You're making me think I'm going craz—"

"—It's my trail name, dude. I don't use my real name on the trail, brother."

"Oh." Brenner had forgotten that serious hikers—at least the most granola of the ragged bunch of mountaineers on the trail—selected trail names. Cultish, in his opinion.

On cue, the man stared Brenner very firmly in the eyes, making the young vet nervously shift his feet, partially due to the stare but also due to the proximity to him that his new acquaintance considered socially acceptable to stand, and asked, "What's your name?" His eyes glistened as the words came from his mouth, with much anticipation for Brenner's response.

Shit. Mind reeling, searching for the right name to say, and *extremely* hesitant to use his real name in response to Sticks, Brenner felt he in this moment had to select a "Trail Name".

"Flames!" he blurted out of nowhere. It sucked and he knew it, but he had to act confident, like the name imparted his very essence to its hearer, who at this moment was a man—in Brenner's opinion—one traumatic experience from being a serial killer.

"DUDE!" Sticks shouted loudly, spitting in Brenner's face.

Ignore it. Just hang in there.

"I… effing… LOVE IT. Flames? Is it plural because there are two of you?" he asked excitedly, looking back and forth from Sam to Brenner, so quickly it almost made Brenner nauseous.

"Uhm, yeah! Of course!"

"You know, man, you can't have flames without…"

Oh God.

"STICKS! Gnarly, brother. Mad respect."

Nervous laughter. "Yeah man, I'm glad you like it. It took quite some time to come up with."

"I bet, dude." Sticks looked around to make sure no one else was on the completely desolate trail in the middle of nowhere before saying, "Look, I don't normally do this, but I got a little trail magic for you. Just a little TM, know what I mean, brother?" He reached into his day pack and pulled out a small baggie that looked like it was filled with mushrooms and a small piece of paper, scribbled upon with the handwriting one would expect from Sticks. "Here, man. In case you need a little pick me up. If you're having a bad day, just eat a little handful and you'll be translocated to a much happier place! Oh, and my number is in there too. When you're done hiking—and take your time, by the way. It's about the journey, dude—maybe ole Sticks and Flames can join up and reminisce on this beautiful day we're sharing here on the trail."

Brenner, feeling it was a good time to start slowly backing away, took the bag, thanked Sticks, and lied. "Yeah, man, maybe we can go get a beer sometime!"

"Eureka, man! A fellow brew-lover! We are pretty similar, you and me." Sticks beamed and slapped his knee.

"For sure, man. I better get going, though. I'm trying to get to Bly Gap by nightfall."

"Oh, easy peasy, man. You just got nine miles of nice and easy walking. There is a stone shelter there too, so you don't have to set up the ole tent. I know sometimes camping gets a little..."

Don't do it.

"...intense. Get it? Intense? Like in tents?" Sticks wheezed heavily as he laughed, which brought on a guttural coughing fit, one Brenner became slightly concerned would be his last. Brenner stood and watched with wide eyes the whole time, not knowing whether he should try to help by slapping him on the back, also concerned it would bestow upon his hand a smell difficult to wash out. And he'd survived large animal husbandry courses. Ultimately, Sticks recovered.

Brenner feigned a laugh. "Alright! Sounds great, Sticks. Thanks for the advice… and for the mushrooms. I'll catch ya later."

"For sure and for certain, Flames."

Brenner awkwardly walked away to the north, paying close attention to his strides, as he felt an uncomfortable gaze on his back until he rounded the next corner and put a stand of oaks between himself and Sticks. Not a dream, but possibly weirder than one. *Flames.* He laughed to himself. He would never be called that again, he hoped.

On the trail once more, Brenner was mostly hiking along the ridgeline in the average direction of North. Around him, the midday sun shone brightly on the sequentially smaller mountains and hills to his left and right. He was happy to see the day looked to be mostly clear, with only occasional cumulonimbus clouds passing between him and the sun, giving small moments of relief from the heat. He would rather be hot than soaking wet and shuddered when he thought of the preceding evening's storm. Sam seemed to feel the same way and smiled between pants when Brenner sat on a log to rest several hours after the encounter with Sticks. Brenner had still not fully recovered from the awkward encounter and the only proof that he was, in fact, awake was the small bag of *Psilocybin cubensis* mushrooms he occasionally fiddled with in his front left pocket.

"These aren't for you, girl," he said to the hound who came over to inspect the bag when he pulled it out to look at the dainty, light-grey caps. Brenner had gone through a phase in college where he partook in marijuana regularly, but had little experiences with drugs otherwise, and had never tried hallucinogenic mushrooms. *I wonder how many you're supposed to eat*, he thought to himself. He couldn't just throw them away, the risk that Sam or some other unsuspecting animal would eat them was too high. He shoved the baggie back into his pocket. Using sweaty hands to open his fold-out trail map, he spread it across his lap and started looking for thin blue lines.

His eyes came to rest on a line with the label "Big John Creek" that looked to be a short distance off the trail from Plumborchard Gap. Although his initial goal was to make Bly Gap by nightfall, he came to the realization that he had no obligation to finish his journey in any specific timeframe. Ben meant what he said, he'd keep his job open for as long as Brenner needed. He was also going to stop by the house regularly to check on things. The lawn service and the mortgage payments would keep auto drafting, and they'd saved up a bit of a nest egg prior to Lily's drowning. Brenner decided he'd find the creek and fish it. *If I don't make Bly Gap tonight, who cares.*

With Sam at his heels he started off again. His mouth tasted of teriyaki jerky, which at this point on the journey was relatively novel and most welcome. A strong pull of water from the tube coming over his right shoulder and he was ready to press forward, no longer towards an eventual end of his journey, but rather towards a small, colorful member of the char family that was likely swimming around a virgin creek deep in the temperate Appalachian rainforest, unaware of Brenner's—or any human's—existence.

"Damn it," Brenner gasped several hours later as he bushwhacked through dense vegetation to the west of the Appalachian Trail towards what he hoped would be Big John Creek. Sam was unable to run ahead through the thick colors of green and followed closely in his footsteps, looking up at him as if to say, "Hey man, the trail was back there." Brenner was careful to strategically break larger limbs as he passed them to leave a trail to follow back to the AT. He chuckled when he looked backwards though, because no breadcrumb trail was needed, and it would be exceedingly obvious exactly where he came from on account of the massive path of foliagicide. He stopped suddenly in his tracks and listened with his mind and his heart when he heard a soft bubbling of water.

"Thank God," he said, looking at Sam. He was starting to doubt the validity of his map and even the existence of creeks in general. Thirty feet forward along his blazed trail, the vegetation transitioned from smaller hardwood trees to a true riparian ecosystem, evidenced by the dense thicket of rhododendron, through which flowed a gentle, slightly off-colored creek.

"Well, if it isn't Big John." Brenner found a small opening through which to crawl to access the creek. Sam particularly loved this discovery and bounded through the branches and, much to Brenner's frustration, leapt into the middle of the flowing water. "Sam! OUT!" He pointed to the bank, where a pouting and sighing dog slowly meandered and collapsed in a pile of disappointment, apparently having thought the purpose of all this bushwhacking was for her swim. After a particularly heartbreaking whimper, Brenner snapped off a small branch from a dead oak tree and threw it to her. She quickly forgot about the creek and began vigorously chewing her new toy.

Brenner had packed two fly rods for this trip, which may seem like a waste of space to someone who doesn't fly fish. However, when broken apart and packed in tubes, fly rods are quite small in diameter and are easily stuffed into side pockets of a backpack. Overkill? Maybe, but Brenner wanted options for both small water, which comprised most of the journey along the trail, and big water, as the route should take him across the Pigeon and Nantahala Rivers.

The first and smaller rod was a small two-piece 2wt rod that was less than seven feet long, allowing the caster better maneuverability under heavy rhododendron cover. After pulling the delicate line through each of the guide eyes, he opened a small fly box and picked out a Royal Wulff, a mayfly imitation with a red stripe between what would, for all intents and purposes, be the thorax and abdomen. A classic dry fly pattern that has been rendered relatively obsolete by newer, more realistic patterns would be perfect for these creeks, in Brenner's mind, because these fish had never seen fishing flies before and something with a little flair would catch their eyes. More importantly, it was Brenner's favorite fly.

With a soft crunching of hound teeth on splintering wood and the eternal bubbling of water over riverbed as his background track, Brenner extended the rod forward and pointed at a small eddy underneath foliage on the left side, upstream from where he stood. He figured that's where he would wait for food to come floating down the creek, were he a brook trout. Using his right thumb and pointer finger to grasp the dainty fly, he pulled both it and the loose line back to his right ear, creating a pronounced bend of tension in the small rod. When he released the fly and line, the Royal Wulff shot cleanly through the air towards where he pointed and landed within an inch of where he imagined a fish to be idly swimming.

Immediately his eyes were drawn to movement two feet away from the fly and he watched as what he originally thought was a river stone quickly swam forward and then up in the water column towards the Royal Wulff. It paused, when its snout was less than an inch from the fly and held itself in place with a light flicking of its tail. *Eat it. Eat it. Eat it.*

SPLASH

For such a small fish, merely six inches in length, it aggressively attacked the imitation. Seeing the trout eat his fly and the resultant wiggling of the rod tip shot adrenaline through Brenner's body and made him feel instantly warmer, happier, as if nothing else mattered but that singular moment, deep in the mountains, away from the rest of the world and all its selfish, aimless problems. He looked up through a small gap in the canopy and thanked whoever might be up there listening to him as his hands used muscle memory to pull the fish to his feet. He leaned down, wet his right hand, and gently grasped the fish and pulled him from his world into Brenner's. Small brook trout have tremendously large eyes for the size of their bodies. *What a little frog*, Brenner thought as he chuckled.

The fish's body was breathtaking, adorned with colors Brenner thought incapable of existing through the accepted notion of evolution. He didn't know how the world came to be or what his purpose was in it, especially considering recent events, but he knew someone or something masterfully crafted the brook trout and used the finest tools in doing so.

The base color of deep green was streaked with bronze on the trout's belly. Mixed in with the bronze were hints of strawberry, left over from the spring spawn. The fins were dark with a bright leading edge, like they were dipped in pure, untainted white. Evenly spaced spots dotted its side going from the back of his gill plate to the front of his tail fin. Each spot comprised an outer ring of sky blue with a pinpoint of red orange in the center. As eyes move from the spots up to the fish's dorsum, the spots transition to linear patterns like that on a topographic map, each one meandering in a different direction. When considering that each fish is unique and no two share the same pattern, it takes a large leap of faith to believe brook trout just happened to exist. When there is such beautiful art, there must be an artist. Brenner thanked the artist as he let the fish swim from his hand back to the undercut bank opposite him on the small creek.

With the freedom of mind and soul that only fishing could provide him, Brenner collapsed with a grin on a soft mat of moss next to Sam, who wagged at his joining her. He rubbed her head firmly and let her lick the slime off his hand. "Good girl." She wagged faster. "Did you know that? You are such a good girl."

He then pulled the bag out of his pocket and turned it over several times, studying the small mushroom caps. The whole time he had been fishing, the gift from Sticks had been lingering in the back of his mind. He was hesitant to take any without a chaperone, someone who would remain sober in case of a bad trip. However, a part of him felt as though he had nothing to lose, and he had recently read a book on the beneficial effects of psilocybin on trauma, something he was in no way short of lately.

"Alright, when in Rome. I guess I'll eat half of them…? I don't know." Brenner pinched about half of the delicate mushroom caps with his fingers and brought them to his mouth. With eyes closed he put them in his mouth and started chewing. He was surprised by the bitterness, expecting them to taste like shiitakes, maitakes, or his personal favorite, chanterelles; they most certainly did not. He grimaced at the flavor but swallowed them with minimal effort. *Let's see what this does.*

Minutes later, he pulled another brook trout from the creek and showed it to Sam who seemed to give approval by wanting to lick the fish itself, now longing for the flavor she licked from her dad's hand. "No, ma'am! Don't lick the fish!" Brenner laughed loudly and dropped the fish back into the water to swim away from this newfound horror with haste.

Perception of time was lost slowly, cast by cast, as usually happens when fly fishing. Brenner, however, was overcome by a large wave of nausea, which he understood often happened after eating "cubes". By some miracle, he suppressed it and focused more intently on casting. The first sign that his mental state was changing was three casts in a row that required untangling from the broad, waxy leaves of rhododendron. He decided fishing would soon be futile and began getting the feeling he needed to make his way back towards the larger, better-marked trail before he was seeing sounds and hearing colors.

He called Sam from her newfound bed and pointed ahead, letting her lead the way away from the creek. As his feet left the water, he noticed a slight green haze around all the leaves he brushed past, and reached out to see if he could feel the extra dimension. His fingers moved through the shimmer but felt nothing. The creek continued to bubble behind him, and he became acutely aware it was the most melodious sound he had ever heard. He focused on the forest floor as his feet moved forward, softly squishing the richly brown soil, a substrate he knew to be full of life and the potential for producing everything from grasses to morels to towering hemlock trees. He scooped a small handful and brought it to his face and with an open mouth breathed in the smell of life. Ahead, the opening to the Appalachian Trail let in a window of afternoon light that draped over the roots that ran along the ground like tendrils of direction, pulling him forward.

He glided through the opening, feeling as though he weighed nothing, and turned left to continue his journey, which was now feeling overwhelmingly spiritual. He started jogging, or maybe sprinting—he couldn't tell, and he didn't care. He felt like he could fly if only he spread his wings and allowed the swirling air of the mountains to encase his body and lift him skyward. He went on like this for some time, a confused, but eager hound on his tail, dumbfounded at her owner's newfound vivacity—she had been hoping he'd run with her since they first set foot out of the 4Runner. Brenner squinted to appreciate the essence of every textured trunk, fluttering leaf, and craggy rock as he flew past them, looking at each like it was his first time ever seeing the outdoors, or perhaps like he had lived his entire life blind and had just been gifted sight.

After an unknown quantity of time had passed them by, the two adventurers came to a small wooden bridge that spanned over a trickling spring that was moving with gravity down to their left, likely to dump into Big John Creek at some undiscovered location on the mountainside. No admonition was made this time when Sam went headlong into the water, splashing happily in the warm sunshine, rehydrating herself with gulp after gulp of the pure, if slightly sulfuric, spring.

Brenner realized he was sweating, but only when he looked down at his arms, which seemed to be moving back and forth through his visual field. Thinking he might get overheated without realizing it, the young man followed the hound's lead and joined her in the spring, gently laying backwards until his arms and lower back were resting on river stones, welcoming the refreshing cold. This was simply too much for Sam to handle. With utter ecstasy, she bounded towards him and pounced on his chest, pushing him all the way into dorsal recumbency. He spewed water from his mouth as he laughed and grabbed his dog, beaming at her joy, which was communicable. He pressed his forehead into hers and stroked both sides of her face, causing her feet to dance in place while her rump wagged back and forth. She pulled her head away and pressed her tongue to his chin, running it all the way up to his brow.

At that moment, Brenner realized he had never seen a more beautiful dog and he kept eye contact with her for several moments. "I love the shit out of you, you dumb dog!" She responded by twirling in a circle. Or did she? Brenner looked around and realized that everything seemed to be twirling in circles, and he could almost appreciate outlines of geometric shapes of bright neon colors shifting in his periphery. *Oh boy*, he thought, *maybe I ate too many. Oh well.* He laid back into the spring and enjoyed the warmth of sunshine on his face as he let the opening of the canopy above him, consisting mostly of eastern white pines, start to spin with perfect geometry.

Then something extraordinary happened. Brenner began seeing memories of his life with such clarity it felt like he was reliving them. He was shown moments from his childhood, his mother with her dirty blonde hair and thick-rimmed glasses gently pushing him in the swing set his father built from scratch, while the smell of hamburgers drifted in rolling clouds of smoke from a charcoal grill operated by the swing set builder himself, whose mostly bald head was adorned with a Carolina Panthers ball cap. He turned around, smiled at Brenner and said, "I'm so proud of you…" The words reverberated in the air above the mountain spring as subsequent memories flooded his mind.

As the memories progressed through time, Brenner started feeling a sense of foreboding, as there was a large portion of his life that had of late been replaced by a desperate heart-breaking pain—Lily. *Don't show her to me. Please, I'm begging you, don't show her to me.* His pleadings were futile and soon he was reliving memories of their first date at the small county fair, a week after meeting her at the clinic. Next was Christmas at her parents' house. Then kayaking down the Chattooga River. The moments brought a pure smile to his mouth and soft, tender tears to his eyes. He continued to be trapped in this movie of his love story for over an hour as the sun slowly sank lower in the sky and the day turned from a colorless brightness into a softening orange hue.

Eventually the memories progressed well past the honeymoon phase and then entered the tumultuous reality of their marriage, and he could do nothing but continue bearing witness to the story from this ethereal third-party perspective. The bitterness and resentment the two had begun harboring for each other made him shudder. He saw the way they talked to each other and the desolate nature of their physical love life. Their love, itself, was deep and strong and they merely had problems that most people encounter in marriage. The difference, however, lay in their approach to dealing with their problems.

Rather than seeking help when things took a downward turn, Brenner just spent more time at work. He then was shocked that Lily wasn't madly in love with him when he collapsed on the couch late every night. Her lack of physical touch hurt his feelings and made him feel like less of a man—less *her* man. Lily, for her part, did initially try to get Brenner to seek counseling and therapy for what she perceived to be work-related stress. She failed to understand that the reason Brenner spent so much time at work in the first place was directly due to how she had been propagating their love at home. They still had good moments, but more and more they found themselves bickering, projecting, and moping.

Brenner watched in horror as he truly understood for the first time that the marriage had lost its health and was replaced with a fetid and unreplaceable complacency. Moreover, he began to grasp that the fault mostly resided on him. The world continued to shift around him in colors, though less bright than when the memories were good natured.

A creeping thought started to open the door, a thought that made Brenner wince and hate his own mind. He loathed it with such passion that he began hating himself for even considering letting it enter. But as he had little control of his mind, enter it did.

Maybe what happened was for the best.

Though he staved off vomiting after eating the mushrooms before, this very thought, and moreover, the fact his subconscious lent permission to his mind to think it, caused Brenner to start retching. Now on his hands and knees, he stared at his reflection in the water, pondering the thought that he didn't wish to think, even considering its validity. Of course, he never would have wished for her to die, but he was now aware that for whatever reason, they had trapped each other in a sick marriage.

Thinking was suddenly interrupted by a loud whimper and a frightened bark. Brenner looked up to see Sam take off at a full panicked sprint up the trail. Mildly dazed, Brenner stood up and called her. She didn't stop. Then Brenner heard the soft wingbeat of a bird fly over him in the same direction as Sam. His eyes searched through the shifting colors until he saw the author of the wingbeat. When he found the bird, he gasped and also started running. It was a mockingbird. He looked behind him after a few paces and noticed a bright light moving through the woods in his direction. He looked up and yelled at the bird, thinking to himself, *please don't respond. Please don't talk. I'm not crazy.*

The bird continued flying straight but turned its head and stared into Brenner's soul with a beady, glossy black eye. "Run, Brenner."

Chapter 8

Brenner's heart jumped into his throat at the voice of the bird, the very same from his recurrent nightmare months before. His legs became unbridled, and he ran with all the speed of terror forward along the trail, following the hound, who was now only visible on longer straightaways, which were few and far between. Though the setting sun was to his left, following its westward path across the summer sky, Brenner's shadow was eerily cast forward, being mostly directed by the light that flowed through the forest behind him, painting the trees around him with a bright white glow.

The shifting kaleidoscopic colors he had moments before enjoyed were losing their vivacity and became dulled into washed out versions of their former brilliancy and were eventually replaced with shades of gray and depressing brown, continuing to swirl through Brenner's field of vision. He heard whispering sift through the leaves behind his left shoulder. If he stopped, he thought he might be able to make out the words, but no ounce of his being wanted to stop. A full flood of endogenous epinephrine coursed through his veins as he sprinted ahead.

The mockingbird had caught up with Sam and called back, saying, "This way, Brenner! It hurts the trees. It hurts the trees." A deep groaning from behind Brenner responded to the bird.

"Sam!" Brenner yelled through heavy panting. "Here, Sam!" He began to realize his dog was leaving him behind and would soon be out of sight entirely. Frustrated and terrified tears streaked down Brenner's cheeks as his mind wrestled with his current reality.

Am I dreaming?

No sooner had the thought crossed his mind than Brenner's foot caught on a meandering oak root that snaked across the trail. His velocity flung him through the air and his arms moved in erratic, bracing loops until he crashed into the firmly packed dirt on the trail.

Blood oozed from fresh scrapes on his hands and the accompanying pain cemented in his brain the dreadful affirmation that he was indeed awake. As he struggled to regain composure and find equilibrium through the altered reality that was his world, the hairs on his neck started standing up and the air around him was replaced by a cold draft.

"Brenner, let me see you…"

The breathy voice followed the trail and moved the branches of the hemlocks and pines that bordered the path. His blood grew cold to match the air. He knew that voice, or at least some semblance of it, like he'd heard it thousands of times. This bestowed no comfort and rather than remaining on the ground to meet its author, Brenner scrambled to his feet and continued his frantic pace after Sam, terrified he might never see her again.

Brenner outpaced the cold voice of the mountain for a length of time that seemed immeasurable. It could have been ten minutes, or it could have been several hours. He never tired and his feet moved with their own motivation, lungs involuntarily filling and emptying, heart racing but never giving up. Sweat wicked away into the ghastly draft that encircled him from behind as quickly as it escaped his pores. Brenner felt as though he had been running his whole life, that no living existed prior to this moment, and that he would run until the time in which his clock ran out.

His vision continued to shift with dark, natural colors, making the mountain seem like an amoebous, sentient lifeform beckoning him forward. However, he became acutely aware of the darkening of the sun and the lack of any shadow preceding his movement. The voice was gone. The light was gone. The night was quiet. *Where am I? Where is Sam?* He stopped and rested his hands on his knees and breathed heavily, finally starting to feel shades of exhaustion. Tears began falling to the forest floor and he looked at them curiously, finally realizing they were coming from his eyes. He gave into sadness and howled into the night around him, like a mourning wolf who had lost its pup. The howl echoed through the valleys, disturbing any ears unlucky enough to perceive it. Anguish and misery were layered thickly over exhaustion, anger, and hopelessness.

When finally, Brenner decided to walk forward at a subdued and helpless pace, he was shocked to see a stone shelter illuminated by the moon around the first bend of the trail. Next was a sign that read "Bly Gap". He had run over eight miles in delirium. There would be no finding Sam tonight in the absence of sunlight and, moreover, energy. Brenner's mental capacity had been stolen by psilocybin and the panicked pursuit, and he could barely stumble the twenty paces to the shelter. He hung his head and walked through the old wooden doorway, beginning to remove the pack that he had just remembered was affixed to his back. Tender blisters on his shoulders continued the process of sobering him up.

As he neared the back right corner of the structure he suddenly paused as his eyes caught movement along the ground. He'd failed to check the shelter for wildlife that might have taken up residence. He took a single step back, preparing to make for the door. The creature stood and moved towards him quickly. Moonlight from the window to his left fell on two almond-brown eyes and soft, blue-ticked fur. Brenner burst into uncontrollable tears as he collapsed on the floor and was playfully attacked by his best friend. Both man and dog whimpered into the silent Appalachian night as he held Samantha tightly against his body.

"I thought—" he continued crying, "—I had lost you." Sam whined and licked the salty tears from his face.

The kind of exhaustion that descends in the wake of one relinquishing all adrenaline and, moreover, depleting their mind's finite store of endorphins with hallucinogens seems to pull the conscience from the head down through the body towards the feet and the unmovable ground that lies beneath. As Brenner lay with his best friend, he felt his thoughts begin to surrender to gravity and his body melted to the floor of the small stone shelter. He didn't care—or much less, notice—that the evening was quite cool. His eyes closed at some unknown time, and he found himself focusing on breathing, praying that his body wouldn't somehow forget to contract the fibers of his diaphragm, pulling air into his chest. Eventually Brenner fell asleep, and he in fact continued to breathe without conscious effort.

***

"Brenner, honey, wake up. Come be with me."

Brenner opened his eyes and found himself lying in his honeymoon bed across from Lily, sun-kissed—perhaps sunburned—legs and feet sliding softly against the cool bamboo sheets as he stretched and released the nighttime tension from all the layered muscle bellies in his legs.

"Lilith Miles," Brenner whispered across the bed with a groggy, waking voice. At saying her name, a strange feeling passed over Brenner, like a shade of unplaceable doubt. He shook his head and blamed an acutely realized caffeine deficit. After all, he had finished quite a few liquor drinks in the pool the preceding day.

"Are you ready to go get some breakfast? I want one of those omelets again. I might even ask them to add some fish to mine." Brenner looked up when she finished speaking, as he hadn't thought she liked fish.

After getting dressed, Brenner took his new wife by her hand and started towards the door. "Lily, your hand is ice cold."

"No, it isn't!" she exclaimed, almost irately and yanked her hand out of his grasp, plunging it into her pocket as he opened the door. A moist mountain breeze, smelling faintly of rain and some far-off fire, blew through the frame and swirled through each of the newlyweds' hair.

Mountains. We are in the mountains, *Brenner thought to himself. He could not escape this feeling that they had already had their honeymoon at some point in the distant past. His mind remembered a salty breeze and the smell of the ocean. But why?*

"Let's go!" Lily took off skipping down a stone path towards a small cabin at the end of the driveway that currently had little billows of smoke rolling from its modest stone chimney. The smell of bacon and sausage greeted them both as they walked onto the porch and approached the door. Lily pushed the door open and then pulled him in behind her. To Brenner's surprise, the inside of the cabin looked identical to their home. But wait, we don't have a home yet. Brenner started slowly backing towards the door, feeling fear well up in his stomach. Lily stood in the kitchen by the stove and was smiling at her husband. Suddenly, she gasped, "I forgot about the pizza!" and opened the oven.

On the middle rack of the oven, where Brenner expected to see a burnt pizza, a small creature bounced back and forth. A mockingbird. It looked directly at Brenner, whose blood turned to ice, and shook its head deliberately back and forth. No. No. No.

"Oh! How'd you get in there, silly?" Lily asked as she reached for a large knife on the counter. Brenner turned and ran towards the door, finding it locked. As he fumbled with the knob, his peripheral vision revealed that the bird flew out of the smoking oven to attack Lily, circling her and trying to peck at her eyes. She frantically swung the knife at the bird, producing a guttural scream with each flash of her arm. She turned to Brenner, her eyes locking onto his in a way that made it impossible for him to break contact. "Stay with me, Brenner! Stay with me forever! Don't leave me! Stay with me!"

***

Brenner awoke in a panic the next morning as he was vigorously shaken back and forth. He yelled in alarm when he realized someone had a firm grasp of each of his shoulders.

"It's okay! Hey, man, you're okay! It's just a dream!"

"Who are—where am—what's going on?!" His eyes adjusted to the blue-grey haze of morning light passing through dense clouds of mist slowly rising from the waterways far below the ridgeline and he looked up to see the young black man from the outfitter store the morning he started hiking. "You?"

"Hey man, I told you I'd see you up here at some point… just didn't expect to find you like this. What's going on? Are you hurt? Why didn't you set up a camp?"

Brenner's mind slowly turned over from neutral into drive and he remembered where he was and, unfortunately, what happened the night before. "Brenner," he mumbled, quietly as he rose to his elbows and looked past the doorless frame into the sunrise that was starting to set ablaze the ridge to their east.

"I love your name. Does it have any special meaning?"

"No. I think my parents just liked it. Anyway, what's your name?"

"I'm Rami," the new acquaintance said with a smile. "I know, it's kind of unique too." Rami let the silence linger for a moment as he looked Brenner up and down, making note of the state of his clothes, partially torn, and caked with dirt. "So, what happened to you?"

"I uh… I think I was being—" Brenner stopped and thought about his words, worried he would sound insane if he repeated the story to Rami, "—I had a bad mushroom trip, I think." He looked away from Rami to the stone floor where his hands lay rested open, as if he were praying. He studied the weathered lines that branched back and forth on his palms and finally rubbed them together.

"Must have been real bad," Rami responded with a chuckle. "Did you discover something about yourself that you didn't too much care for, Brenner?"

"Something like that. It was also my first time, and I think I ate too many."

"Well, how many did ya eat?"

Brenner held up his hand to express "wait just a second" and began fumbling around in his pocket until he found what he was looking for. Knowing half of the mushrooms were still in the plastic bag, Brenner presented the remaining contents to Rami and responded, "About this much."

"Hold up, let me look at that." Rami's eyes squinted as he leaned in to see exactly what "this much" meant. When he saw the pile of mushrooms in the back, he staggered backwards in dramatic fashion, put his hand on his belly, tilted his head back and bellowed laughter intermixed with words that Brenner thought must have been a stream of consciousness. Finally, Rami produced decipherable words. "About this much, he says!" He threw his head back and laughed again, only this time without the same amount of air, filling the stone shelter with wheezing. Brenner couldn't help but start laughing himself. He took his hat off and skipped it across the room, watching it bounce off the opposite wall. He made eye contact with Rami, and they continued chuckling for a few seconds until they both caught their breath.

"Good God almighty… Hey buddy, I think you may have figured it out by now, but that's a lot of damn mushrooms. I only ever ate those things once, and let me tell ya, six or seven caps had me eating cookies with my dead grandmama. I bet you *were* tripping!"

"Well, it wasn't my dead grandmother, but I saw some shit, man." Brenner smiled and breathed a partial sigh of relief as it became more apparent the horrifying events of the previous night may have been nothing more than a bad trip on a potent hallucinogen.

"THIS much…" Rami laughed again.

"Okay, okay, I get it now." Brenner rolled his eyes and then looked back at Rami. Initially wanting to complete the entire journey with only Sam, Brenner had newfound appreciation for the idea of a companion. "You want to hike together today?"

"I was about to ask you the same," Rami responded.

"Alright, well let's get to it." Brenner looked around, first at his dog and then at the backpack laying propped against the side wall. "Fortunately, I don't have all that much to pack up."

After stepping out of the shelter, his eyes were drawn to a gnarled oak tree whose split lower trunk hugged the ground closely before shooting upward at a sharp right angle. The branches, a mix between live and dead, sprawled outward from the tree's base, reaching skyward, like it was on its knees, begging for mercy. Mercy from what? For being hideous? For being broken?

Brenner found the tree beautiful. He empathized with it, stripped of its previous easy beauty. The tree, like himself, once stood upright amongst its peers, tall enough likely to feel the warm rays of the sun. Now, it had been reduced to a half-prone posture of defeat, struggling to photosynthesize, drowning in a forest of trees that had known less trauma. *It's just a tree,* Brenner thought, shaking his head. But somehow it was a lot more.

An hour later, Rami and Brenner walked side by side across an open knob, enjoying the gentle breeze that flowed through the grass like waves in a green ocean, staving off an appreciable fraction of the impending summer heat. "Where are you from?" Brenner asked, as he kept an eye on Sam, who frolicked in the grass looking for anything worth sniffing.

"I've moved around quite a bit, but I call Clemson, South Carolina home."

"Oh, did you go to school there?" Brenner asked, knowing it was said to be a similar campus to his alma mater, Auburn.

Rami laughed and replied, "Nah man, I didn't go to Clemson. I was born there but ended up going to South Carolina State on a band scholarship. I went to a few Clemson games with my dad growing up because he got free tickets for working concessions. I'll never forget the first time I saw S.C. State's drumline at halftime of a Clemson game. My dad says I didn't blink once the whole twenty minutes. All I can remember is thinking I wanted to be out there one day. The next week I spent every dollar I made the previous summer on a drum set from a pawn shop. Years later, I found myself out there, hoping to be an inspiration for another young boy."

"Did you ever play with anyone outside of school?" Brenner asked.

"I played in my church on the weekends."

"I bet that was boring compared to the drumline…"

"Brenner, you never been to a black church, have you?"

Rami said, laughing. "Mrs. Jones woulda had my butt if I didn't play like it was a football Saturday. Some of my best playing was in front of the fifty or so members of a spirit-led congregation."

"My apologies! I stand corrected." Brenner laughed.

"Are you a churchgoer?" Rami said, stopping to catch his breath, as Sam came bounding back across the field towards them.

"Uhm, yeah, you know… I used to go with my parents some, growing up."

"Yeah, but are *you* a churchgoer?" Rami asked an uncomfortable Brenner.

Oh boy, this might be a long hike, Brenner thought to himself.

"Well, I suppose not," he finally replied, looking at his feet. "I talk to God when I fish."

"Fair enough. I was just wondering. Where are you from, anyway?" Rami asked, changing the subject.

"Near Greenville," Brenner responded quietly, trying to suppress the emotions clawing at the back of his throat. *Do I tell him why I'm here? Do I tell him about Lily? No.*

The hours passed quickly that day, each moment filled with thoughtful conversation, ranging from previous camping trips to childhood hilarities. Before the two of them realized it, they had hiked all the way to Carter Gap, just under fifteen miles from where they had started that morning. Wanting to sleep under the stars and feeling like he would be wasting the effort on carrying his tent if he chose to only sleep in shelters, Brenner forewent the small wooden planks and shingled roof of Carter Gap shelter, finding a soft, flat spot on the ground.

He collapsed onto an old oak stump next to his tent, when he finally retired his feet for the evening and watched as Rami quickly nursed a few licking flames into a fully birthed fire, sending sharp crackles and hisses into the darkening night. Stiff hiking boots were shed, and the young vet stared at his blistered toes, as if he were asking them why they were blistered. They didn't respond, but rather stuck up awkwardly off the ends of his feet, pruned, moist, and pale, casting giant toe shadows onto the trees that huddled around the clearing behind Brenner.

Rami noticed the staring contest between Brenner and his appendages and said, "Hey bud, I'll get you some moleskin. I brought a bunch."

When he was done, Brenner relaxed on his stump and sipped brown liquor from his flask.

"Rami, do you fish?"

"I won last year's church-wide fishing contest."

"Oh, hell yeah. I knew I liked you," Brenner said, shaking off the chuckle-inducing images of who he figured might have entered a church fishing contest. "You ever try fly fishing?"

"No sir, I have not."

"Well, you're going to tomorrow. I couldn't decide which rod I wanted to use, so I packed my normal one and a shorter one I bought for creeks."

Lily,

I'm in the middle of the woods right now, trying to find some version of sleep. Snoring twenty feet away from me is a new friend. You would be proud of me—you always wanted me to make more friends. His name is Rami, and I think he's the only person with a name weirder than mine. I was lonely before he walked up on me, and I'm glad for his company.

Do you remember our wedding night? I thought you were going to kill Adam after he dropped the wedding cake. I don't know who ever thought it was a good idea for him to carry it. God save that man's future children. When you knelt next to me to start wiping up the overpriced frosting, I was scared to look at you. I didn't want to see evidence on your face that any part of the night was ruined. I wanted it to be perfect. You deserved perfect. Do you remember what you said? The corners of your mouth started twisting upward and you said, "Whatever, we're still married, aren't we?" Next thing I knew, you had tackled me and threw cake on my face. Cake from the FLOOR, *I might add. The bridesmaids watched in horror, likely imagining how they would have reacted if some dumb oaf had dropped their wedding cake. Not you, Lily. You were different from the rest of the girls there—from the rest of the girls anywhere. I fell in love with you so hard it hurt. I felt like you were somehow hand-crafted to be mine.*

I miss you. I keep thinking about you. There is something I must tell you, though. I have been having bad dreams about you. I don't know why, or what they mean. If you have any control over my dreams, which I doubt you do, please help them be more positive. I don't want to forget the good. Help me remember the good.

Love, Brenner

Chapter 9

A full moon painted the rolling landscape with a soft blue while the two companions slept. Every now and again, a dark shadow would creep up and down the slopes, following the path of the soft clouds hanging from the sky, pulled as if by strings from west to east, searching for the sun that would surely come. Gentle snoring, emanating softly from each of the tents, was quietly suppressed by the sounds of the living forest. A blithe pack of coyotes yipped and howled to each other from across the nearest valley. Two barred owls noisily hooted their four-beat "who cooks for youuuuu…" Crickets and frogs sang to each other, competing to be the louder species. One might have even sworn they heard a cougar's ghastly screech come screaming down the mountainside. Brenner and Rami, however, heard none of it and slept until the Earth rotated enough to call forth a purple sunrise.

"Morning," Brenner said lazily, as he climbed from his tent and started water to a boil for a morning cup of coffee, wishing he had packed caffeine pills to save him from the extra effort.

"Good morning." Rami methodically stowed camp back into his pack. He then sat and gladly accepted the mug from Brenner. "I should have brought NoDoz."

"No shit, man. That's hilarious, I was just thinking the same thing." Brenner laughed.

"So, Brenner," Rami started, lowering the mug to his lap, "tell me about Lily."

Brenner was mid-sip when the words arrived, and he spewed hot coffee onto his lap and the surrounding dirt. "What did you just say?" he asked after a brief coughing fit.

"Lily. Who is it? You shouted her name in your sleep a few times. It sounded like a nightmare."

"You got anywhere you gotta be? This is liable to take a few minutes," Brenner responded with a chuckle, studying the unique pattern of coffee splattered on the ground around him.

"Believe it or not, I got nothing but time."

"Lily was my wife, Rami."

"Oh, I'm sorry man. You're divorced…"

"No. I'm widowed. Lily died about two months ago, drowned in a river in Charleston." His eyes stung and he rubbed them with gritty hands, trying to keep moisture within the lids.

"Damn," Rami said, as he too quietly stared at the ground. "I don't know what to say, Brenner. I—I can't imagine."

"As a kid, I used to have crushes on girls at school, ya know?" Brenner said, looking up at his companion. "I can't count them all with all my fingers and toes. And every one of them somehow broke my middle school heart, as much as a middle schooler can understand heartbreak. Being stood up at a homecoming dance, seeing a crush kiss my best friend, being made fun of for bringing someone flowers on Valentine's Day. But my mom, man—" Brenner said, now through tears, "—my mom used to say 'Don't worry. One day a girl will see you the way I see you. One day a girl will love every little thing about you. You won't have to try so hard, and you will be thankful all these other girls turned you down.' She promised me that after every single one of them." He paused and watched a tear fall to join the expelled coffee. "That was Lily. Lily was that girl for me. And now that girl is gone. I can't even tell her how much I miss her. She has no idea." He paused for a moment before continuing, somberly, "We had been fighting more and more before she died. It's complicated, but I honestly think it was my fault. I avoided conflict and instead spent all my time at the clinic, which obviously only made things worse. I would give anything in the world to hold her and tell her how much she means—meant—to me."

"I'm sure she knows. I guess that's why you're out here, huh?"

"Yeah, I needed to clear my mind. See how well it's working?" Brenner laughed through the tears. Rami softly laughed with him before walking over and extending his hand.

"Come on, Brenner. Let's walk the sorrow away."

"If you're up for it, church boy, I'm planning on fishing the sorrow away today."

"As long as you promise getting out-fished won't add to the sorrow."

"I'll buy you a case of beer if you out-fish me, Rami." Brenner allowed himself to be pulled to his feet. When he turned around, in place of his tent sat his backpack, loaded and ready for hiking. *When did he pack that?* Brenner looked curiously at Rami.

"You took a long time to brew that coffee, and I don't plan on waiting on your ass all morning. Apparently, we have some fish to catch."

***

"You don't have to cast it back and forth so much," Brenner said an hour up the trail from camp. They had happened upon a small wooden bridge spanning fishable water. A dainty mayfly, golden in color, drifted out of the slight morning breeze and landed on Brenner's arm, morning sunlight passing halfway through its feathery, semi-translucent wings, which it held in a perfect triangle above its slender body. "That's called false casting and it's what everyone does in the movies. There are too many trees here for that, and you'll be catching nothing but rhododendrons. Just let the water take it—like this." Brenner let the small bubbling creek pull his fly downstream until it was about ten yards away, twisting and turning against the current as it bounced on the water's surface, inches to the right of a half-exposed river stone. "Then you just flip it forward with one motion. Watch how the water loads the line for you." With a graceful motion, Brenner sent the dry fly darting forward through the wet, summer air.

"Ah... Okay, I think I get it now. Let me try." Rami repeated the same motion as Brenner had and the result was far more beautiful. By chance or by grace, Rami's fly landed on a small eddy immediately off the left bank, somehow gliding under a bundle of waxy green leaves that was less than a foot from the water's surface. Before the water even noticed something had landed on it, a sharp splash engulfed Rami's fly. Dumbfounded, with mouth agape, Brenner watched as Rami set the hook and quickly but smoothly stripped in his fly line to bring the fish into the palm of his hand.

"A brown trout," Brenner mumbled, staring at the fish. "I didn't know..." His voice trailed off. He looked back and forth from Rami to the fish. "I didn't know there even were brown trout up here." Brown trout were Brenner's favorite to catch, commonly known as a trophy fish to most fly anglers. The color of butter, brown trout are adorned with bright red spots, intermixed with black speckling. Wild brown trout, like the one squirming in Rami's gentle grip, have an almost translucent blue shadow spot on their gill plate, behind their eye. "Who are you?" Brenner asked a laughing Rami. "I'm serious. I couldn't have made that cast, and I've been doing this for years."

"I told you. I won the church fishing contest."

"Maybe I *should* start going to church."

"Hey, just think about it, man, Jesus said to be fishers of men. I like to think it helps to know how to be fishers of fish first."

Brenner rolled his eyes. "What, did Jesus tell you to cast to the *other* side of the stream or something?"

Rami laughed. "Oh, a Bible joke, huh? I guess you *were* raised in the church."

The small trout was unamused by the religious jokes and continued wiggling back and forth in Rami's hand, wondering if it would ever again feel water flowing through its gills. The two fishermen noticed the fish's rhythmic, but in vain, buccal pumping as its blood slowly exhausted the stored oxygen. Rami lowered the trout headfirst into the water and gently held its tail until it started swimming away from them back to the eddy, fully revived. Rami had asked about keeping the trout for dinner, but Brenner made it clear he didn't keep trout unless he was fishing with spinning tackle. Besides, they both had plenty of food, albeit freeze-dried meals.

"Now it's your turn," Rami said to Brenner, raising his eyebrows and subtly lowering his chin in challenge.

Sam had been idle long enough and charged chaotically into the stream, bounding between the two men, soaking what dry clothes they still wore. Brenner closed his eyes and sighed, knowing splashing hounds don't typically attract trout. She had, however, behaved exceptionally all morning and deserved to be rewarded with a swim.

***

"That's peculiar." Brenner and Rami had continued their trek into the early afternoon, pausing only for water and handfuls of jerky, the flavor of which started losing its appeal as the novelty wore off. Brenner had stopped in the middle of the trail and was staring off into an open stand of pines rising from a soft floor of fallen needles that choked additional growth.

"What's peculiar?" Rami responded, walking the five paces back to his new friend.

"That tree…" Brenner continued staring, now cocking his head ever-so-slightly to the side. "It looks like a person. I mean—it looks like a woman. Do you see it? Right there!" He pointed out into the forest.

Rami walked behind Brenner so that he could follow the line of sight that started at Brenner's eyes and extended out past the end of his index finger. After studying every tree in the vicinity of the point, Rami replied, "No. I don't see anything but pine trees."

Brenner looked at Rami in confusion and then back to where he was pointing. "It's right—wait..." The tree was no longer there. In fact, there was nothing there except pine needles and a cluster of flowers somehow pushing through the straw. "It's... gone." Brenner breathed deeply as his brain tried to process the sudden absence of something he knew he had seen. A bead of cool sweat dripped from the curls creeping out from under his hat and followed gravity down to the small of his back, where it caused him to suddenly shiver.

"You good, man?" Rami asked.

"Yeah, I just... I know I saw—never mind, let's keep walking."

"You sneak some more of those mushrooms when I wasn't looking?" Rami joked.

Brenner laughed shortly and responded, "Not a chance. I'm not touching the rest of those. I think I'm going crazy."

"You've been through a lot. The mind is a funny thing, Brenner."

The two of them continued walking up the trail, but Sam lagged, still sitting next to where Brenner had paused. "Come on, girl!" Brenner called his best friend. Sam's hackles stood on end, and she produced a low, guttural growl before finally turning to follow them. *Is she going crazy too?*

"Ugh, not again," Brenner moaned as he looked at the heavy clouds rolling in from the west. Angled streaks of gray mottled the green of distant mountainsides and the air began to smell of rain.

"A little water never hurt anybody," Rami replied.

"Yeah, tell that to all the people who've drowned."

"Oh," Rami responded, frowning.

Thirty minutes later a wave of white noise, brought by millions of droplets of rain hitting the canopy climbed up the side of their mountain, following a sustained gust of wind that ran through Brenner's hair. Sam, inspired by the excitement of the changing weather, forgetting her fear of thunder, jumped, and spun in the air. Brenner and Rami found a dense grove of mountain laurel, under which they waited out the transient summer storm. No thunder this time, thankfully.

"Alright, favorite food?" Rami asked, almost surprising Brenner by breaking the silence, if one could call that heavy white noise of a downpour silence.

"Fish."

"What kind?"

"Any and all, my friend," Brenner responded.

Rami smiled at being called Brenner's friend. "I guess that makes sense. I still can't believe you never keep the trout you catch."

Brenner shook his head. "I keep the fish I catch at the grocery store, because if I don't, someone else will. The fish in the creeks—I just might be able to catch them again one day, so I let them go." Rami shook his head, in obvious disapproval. The rain started to slow. "What about you?" Brenner asked.

"Carolina barbecue. Mustard based," Rami said, staring up into the heavens as if he might be able to summon barbecue, like heavenly manna of old. "Brisket, in particular."

"Now there is something we can agree on," Brenner responded, following Rami's gaze, also praying for barbecue to fall from the sky. He imagined a slice of beef, covered in a dark, crunchy, sauce-laden bark, under which lay a layer of juicy, mouth-watering fat. His stomach growled. "How ambitious are we feeling right now?" he asked, looking down from Heaven to his new friend. "It looks like we are just shy of Albert Mountain." He studied the map, turning it on its side, to orient the map in the direction of the trail next to where they sat.

Knowing precisely what Brenner was getting at, Rami responded, "I don't feel like hiking much farther. Let's find a place to set up camp once this shower passes." Brenner sighed in relief and nodded.

"It's all soaked," Brenner said later, once their tents were erected and all that was left to do that day was stoke a fire and rehydrate a combination of beef and mac and cheese—almost as delicious as beef brisket. Knowing the first few days of the trail would not swing near a town to restock, Brenner had packed heavily. Moreover, his sorrow suppressed his appetite, and he had at least three days of food left.

Depending on how ambitious they were feeling the following day, they might make it to Winding Stair Gap where the trail crossed Highway 64, and more importantly, the nearby town of Franklin, to which they could catch a shuttle to resupply, shower, and even sleep in a motel if they wanted the comfort of a bed.

"Find a standing dead tree. It'll have dried off faster," Rami said, as he started leaning small sticks against each other like a teepee in their makeshift fire ring.

Brenner raised his eyebrows in admission of the good idea and wandered off into the woods with his hound. A hundred yards from camp, Sam shot through the dense underbrush into a clearing that was not visible to Brenner, who resented the idea of bushwhacking. He eyed a small, bare pine that leaned against another tree with the weight of death. The other tree stood soberly but healthy with bright green needles and thick, dark brown, layered bark, creating a stark comparison between living and deceased. Brenner shuddered, as the sight made his stomach uneasy. Memories—too many of them—began creeping up his spine and into the subconscious reaches of his cerebrum. *Will I ever be rid of this sorrow?*

Brenner's attention was snapped away from the present, somber scene by the sound of Sam's howls screaming through the woods like a freight train. One after another, the howls ran together, expressing canine emotion somewhere between fear and anger, like a panicked wrath. Brenner could tell Sam was hot on something's trail, sprinting from his right to left, through the supposed clearing, at an angle slightly away from camp.

"SAM!" Brenner shouted, as he started jogging towards the sound of her barking, still unable to get through the brush and into the clearing. "Samantha! Here, girl! Come here! SAM!" Worried she had jumped a black bear with cubs, Brenner's mind started showing him his life without the dog, something he wasn't sure he could handle. At that moment, Sam seemed to whimper, but fortunately he could hear her moving back towards him. Moments later, she exploded from the brush and high-tailed it back towards camp. Relieved that she looked unharmed, but also now concerned she was fleeing something, Brenner followed and chased behind her.

"Are you both okay?" Rami asked loudly, meeting them at the edge of the woods next to the campsite.

"Yeah, I think so. Sam must have jumped a bear or something." They both quietly listened for what could have been a couple of minutes, to ensure nothing was pursuing. Crickets. Nothing more.

"That dog will be the death of me," Brenner gasped, realizing how out of breath he was after his brief sprint through the woods. "Where did she go, anyway?"

"She's sitting by the fire now."

"Oh, good, I know she was wet from running through the—wait, the fire? You've got one going already? How?"

"I guess the wood wasn't that wet after all." Rami shrugged.

Here I thought I *was skilled at camping.* Brenner stared at his dog, who shook out her coat and steamed next to the crackling and hissing wood, ablaze in the ring.

Brenner made Sam sleep at his feet that night, on account of her damp fur in the cooling Appalachian evening. She realized her lot after the third denied attempt to nestle into the sleeping bag with her owner, and finally collapsed in moping defeat at the bottom of the tent.

Brenner tossed and turned most of the night, getting no more than an hour of sleep at a time, mind occupied by a combination of present and past nightmares mixed with the oddities of the trail thus far. As much as he wanted to feel the healing of his mind and heart, the strange feeling he was not alone on the trail pressed firmer on the forefront of his mind. Eerie feeling turned to conscious thought. Had it been a singular bad trip, an isolated tree in the woods, or one chase by his dog through the forest, maybe he could attribute it to happenstance. The combination of all of them produced fear. He sincerely wished he hadn't touched Sticks' 'shrooms and wondered if he was having flashbacks. Regardless, any remaining chance of ignoring these incidents vanished when he opened his notebook to journal the following morning in the pale light of daybreak.

"Good morning, girl," he said groggily to his dog as Sam stretched lazily, looking at him with an air of annoyance for keeping her up all night with his restlessness. Nothing a belly rub couldn't fix. Brenner yawned and reached into his backpack to retrieve the small leatherbound journal he'd been using to write to Lily's memory.

Brenner rubbed some of the sleep from his eyes as he opened the journal to flip to the next blank page. He paused when he reached the entry from the day before and sighed, on account of the nightmares that persisted seemingly indefinitely. When finally, Brenner turned the page, his body was gripped by a cold panic. He shuddered and let out an involuntary gasp as the journal fell from his hands, landing with a soft thud on the tent floor.

Chapter 10

Come find me, Bren. You know where to look…

With his heart beating firmly at the base of his throat, increasing in rate every passing second, Brenner closed and opened the journal three or four times, hoping each time the page would be blank. He smacked the side of his face to ensure he was awake. No matter what he did, the words remained on the page in unmistakable handwriting—Lily's.

Brenner's world started spinning and his ears began to ring, louder and louder until it seemed to sharply sting his brain. He collapsed forward and let his hands brace him, breathing deeply and intentionally, feeling his vision begin to blur at the periphery. Seeing her owner in a state of distress, Sam crawled to his side and shoved her soft muzzle into his armpit and then against his neck. He reached out with one hand and grabbed a patch of fur on her neck scruff, clinging to some part of reality that wasn't slipping away towards subconsciousness. Sam grounded Brenner in the moment long enough for him to feel the spinning begin to slow and the ringing started to dissipate. He grabbed Sam and collapsed on the floor with her, spooning her and petting the hair under her axillae. She licked his face, thankful her owner seemed to be recovering.

He opened the journal and read the words repeatedly, now thinking about what they could mean. *Am I going crazy?* was his first thought. Though disturbing, that thought wasn't productive. Even if he was going crazy, what could he do about it now? He was deep on the Appalachian Trail, away from civilization and the comforts of the world. Regardless of his mental state, this horror needed to be addressed. He couldn't continue hiking like this, with newfound haunting phenomena making themselves known daily. *Lily. Could it really be her?*

With his recent dreams and experiences Brenner wasn't sure he wanted to find Lily, even if it was her. Had she heard his thoughts the other day… about her death being somehow fortunate? After all, that's when the first haunting seemed to occur, if you discounted his experience the night she died. Could he discount it? On the other hand, he was never able to tell her goodbye. He had been writing to her in his journal almost daily. He *wanted* to talk to her. He had been longing for it, like a netted fish longs for water. A hopeless rent in his heart existed that could be filled with nothing other than telling Lily how he truly felt and even apologizing, something until now he had considered impossible. The longer he pondered, the more his thoughts and emotions transitioned from fear to desire. He ached for her.

Additionally, he suppressed the ever-growing concern that perhaps he was not mentally sound and that at this point he might need to be in a psych ward. At the end of the day, he didn't want to leave the trail and give up on whatever this journey was leading him towards.

"I'll be right back, girl. Stay here." Brenner slowly zipped his tent back up from the outside as he spoke softly to the blue-ticked companion that panted with apprehension from the inside. Brenner looked to the east and saw that the sun had not yet crested the soft ridgeline. It was just past shooting light, and far earlier than they usually started hiking. He paused to listen for any noise coming from Rami's tent. Nothing. With a deep breath and a shudder to rid the morning bite of cold, Brenner turned in the direction of his nighttime escapade. The soft, dew-ridden soil compressed slightly with each step, and he silently walked through the woods, stopping to look once more upon the arborous juxtaposition of life and death that he noticed the previous night. A sign, perhaps.

A few paces later, Brenner came to the dense mountain laurel thicket that seemed to form a partition between himself and an opening, evidenced by the lack of canopy on the other side. To his left, he noticed a small game trail that dissected through the brush. He looked back towards the camp and briefly considered turning around. Chills ran from his ears down to his toes. *I'll regret it if I don't go look.*

With a forceful swallow and a subtle nod, Brenner started along the game trail. A few steps in he noticed the trail accommodated his height and width perfectly, as if it was cut for his precise dimensions. He needed not to duck or shimmy. He glided along, making two or three small turns as it wound its way towards the opening on the other side. Brenner began to understand it would not be his first time seeing this clearing. *It's going to be the clearing from my dream.* Feeling like his whole existence was now merely a dream, he continued forward. However, he earnestly hoped he wouldn't see a mockingbird.

The light pouring into the game trail from its end was a different quality than the light he had left behind in the outer world. Bright as midday sun, it forced Brenner to squint as he finally stepped out into the large circular clearing. As his eyes adjusted, he noticed the large stone in the center, and the layered moss in the shape of a man's face. He looked around nervously, unsure what his wife might even look like if she appeared. Seeing nothing resembling Lily, Brenner slowly walked to the center of the ring and sat against the stone.

True silence is difficult to explain, as the explanation itself requires words and sounds. The human body attempts to fill the void, as turbulence of breath elicits noises from nostrils and a beating heart produces a rhythmic soft thud against the inner ear. Thoughts even seem to come to life and the thinker hears their own voice in their mind, overcoming the last ploy of silence. What Brenner experienced in the clearing was otherworldly and was a true, silent void. The silence became loud enough to drown out any noises that would normally be heard in quiet places. The silence had substance and body, and its presence was oppressively draped over everything in the clearing, from the wild grasses on the forest floor to the limbs of the boundary trees that seemed to sag with the weight of nothingness.

The density of the air began to pull at Brenner's mind. At first, the feeling was subtle, and he felt the edges of his wakefulness start extending down his neck and away from his brain, like butter dripping from toast. He shook his head to stave the feeling of sleep. *Drip, drip, drip.* His eyelids began feeling heavy and he struggled with effort to keep them open, trying to maintain a view of his surroundings in this lonely place. With a final effort, Brenner tried to stand. His mind pleaded with his legs to move, but they remained motionless, as if communication from his brain to his extremities was severed. The last of his mental power exhausted, Brenner felt his awareness slide from his head, down through his neck and his torso into the ground beneath him.

Just when he thought he had given in to sleep a bright light emerged from the edge of the clearing opposite where he sat. His eyes opened now with no effort, and he gazed upon the light until it glided to meet him. Slowly the light dissipated and there alone in the clearing Brenner sat face to face with Lilith Miles.

"It can't be," Brenner murmured, taking in the sight of his wife, dressed in a lacy white sundress, the very one she wore on their honeymoon. Her figure seemed to shimmer sporadically, but she was really there in the flesh. She looked just as he remembered, as he always wished to remember her.

"Brenner, my love," Lily said, sweetly. Her voice was kind and as innocent as their first date. Its resonance, depth, and tone awakened a feeling Brenner hadn't felt in months. Love welled in his heart as tears welled in his eyes.

"How… are you here?" he asked, voice quivering. "You died, Lily. I went to your funeral. My baby…" Brenner burst into tears, tears that had been so strongly and willfully suppressed every day since his wife died. His face contorted and he let himself give in to all the emotions of his soul.

"I did die, Brenner. I shouldn't have gone swimming. I shouldn't have gone to the concert. Time is different for me now and I have wished for a thousand years that I had gone with you instead. I wish I had spent every moment with you, as I now have lived lifetimes apart from you. I have searched for you, Brenner. But you weren't ready to be found."

Brenner tried to comprehend Lily's words as he watched her speak. Uneasy, but cursed with the spell of true love, he ignored any feeling of doubt or fear and replaced them with hopefulness and joy. His stomach fluttered with the wing beats of a thousand butterflies. "It's really you… but, how?"

"Don't worry yourself with those thoughts, Bren. You have been living with worry on your mind for too long now. Just know that I'm here with you. I will stay with you as long as you want, my handsome man."

"Lily, my thoughts and dreams about you have been awful lately. They have haunted me almost every day," Brenner responded with a frown. He thought again of the mockingbird and of all the nightmares. "And I just have so much I need to say to you—so much I need to apologize for…"

"Sweetie, that's just the mind's way of healing. If you remember something lost as bad, then the loss won't sting as sharply. It's natural." Her expression became soft and compassionate as she looked at her husband's troubled face. "Do you want me to show you the good?" she asked him, longingly.

"What do you mean?"

"Here, hold my hands, Brenner." She extended her arms towards him.

Brenner stared into her eyes and found a space deep within them that felt like home. He slowly reached out and took her soft hand in his. In that moment, the world around them disappeared and they were both thrust through time back to the memory of their honeymoon on the white shores of an island in the Bahamas.

***

"Hey Carlos, how much longer are we going to be out?" Brenner asked loudly over the sound of the small boat engine and salty Caribbean breeze that rushed through his hair. He looked at his wristwatch and saw that it was around five o'clock. A strong grumble in his belly made him realize he had forgotten to eat lunch, despite the not-so-subtle reminders of his newlywed wife.

The sunbaked Bahamian fishing guide pulled up his oversized sunglasses and responded, "I was gonna show the two a ya one mo spot to look fo bones. That is unless ya done fishin for da day…?"

"Oh, come on Bren, please can we go to one more spot? I only need one more to beat you!" Lily responded, beaming.

Brenner smiled at Lily, pondering to himself how lucky he was to find someone that seemed to love fly fishing as much as, if not more than, he did. "Alright, alright, one more spot. But only if we can order four sushi rolls to split between the two of us when we get back."

"Twist my arm." She winked at him.

Fifteen minutes later, with Carlos in the lead, the three of them walked in a triangle across a shallow sand flat covered with translucent turquoise water, clumps of monkey grass patched in every direction, seemingly to the horizon. The sun was dipping closer each minute to the western intersection of sea and water, casting an orange glow across the surface.

Carlos stopped suddenly and reached down into the water.

"What are you doing?" Lily asked.

"Just going to da grocery store," Carlos said, as his hand emerged with a large conch; it was his dinner for the night.

"Nervous water!" Lily shouted suddenly, referring to the slight turbulence observable on the surface from a school of swimming bonefish, as she pointed to their left.

"Good, Lily!" Carlos responded. "Cast, cast! Put it in front a dem." Lily began false casting with rhythmic eloquence, sending beautiful loops of fly line forward and backward until she had thirty yards of line laid out on the blue water. She let her fly—a shrimp imitation—fall into the water. "Strip, girl, strip!" Carlos said in a frantic voice. Lily aggressively pulled her line back to her in short, fast strips. Resistance to her last strip let her know a bonefish had taken the fly in its mouth. She pulled the line back firmly with her free hand and set the hook. Immediately the line began ripping through the water and any slack disappeared. The drag on her reel screamed as the fish raced in a straight line away from the three of them.

Brenner stood and watched his wife, thinking about all the things he wanted to do with this fisherwoman when they got back to the room that night. After pulling out around a hundred yards of line, the fish finally gave up and allowed itself to be fought back to Carlos's landing net. Lily jumped up and down with excitement when she saw how big the final fish of the day was.

"Now *that's* a bonefish!" Carlos said as he removed the hook. "She put ya to shame, boy," he said with a chuckle to Brenner.

"God, you're so hot," Brenner said to Lily, who blushed.

***

Two hours later, Brenner and Lily were finishing their meal at the sushi shack near the hotel on the beach. Full of sake, they laughed about the memories of the trip so far, like the dog who defecated on Brenner's hat on the beach, and the baby that accidentally punched a sleeping Lily on the airplane.

"I dare you to eat this," Lily said to Brenner, who eyed the spoonful of wasabi that remained on their plate after the sushi had been consumed.

"I'll do it for a kiss."

"Just a kiss…? I could do you one better."

Brenner grabbed the spoon and shoved its contents into his mouth. "See, that's nothing," he said, as his eyes began to water. "Shit, never mind." He started coughing as he felt a searing burn start in his nose and make its way through every sinus. He blinked repeatedly until the burn was gone and reached for the glass to finish the remaining sake.

Lily laughed hysterically as he struggled to breathe. "You idiot. You're such a boy. You'd do anything for sex."

"Guilty as charged," he responded when he finally caught his breath. He noticed Sam Cooke's "Good Times" playing through the old, rusted stereo sitting on a shelf on the patio. "Wait, listen." He paused for a second until Lily recognized her favorite song. "Come on, hooligan!" He grabbed her hand and pulled her from the table onto the white sand of the beach, illuminated by the blue moonlight.

Lilith and Brenner Miles danced the remainder of the evening away to the crackly melodies coming from the nearly retired stereo, against the background noise of small waves cascading in long linear patterns along the beach, starting on the left and ending at an unknown point to their distant right. When finally, the manager of the restaurant unplugged the music, Brenner and Lily collapsed in each other's arms onto the sand and rolled around together. Brenner lay on his back and Lily had him pinned down against the beach, searching his soul. She leaned in and pecked his cheek.

"I love you, Brenner."

He kissed her back passionately and they made love on the sand, not caring who might see, wishing they could both stay in that moment for the rest of their lives.

***

Brenner felt Lily's hands lift from his and suddenly he was back in the half-acre clearing in the mountains. He felt entranced by the memory, now remembering every little detail he had forgotten the last few years, as if it had just taken place the day before. His heart was warm, and his mind buzzed with passion. He looked up at his wife and smiled, but then remembered once more that she had died.

"Oh, Lily," he cried. "Take me back, Lily. I don't want to live in a world without you. I wished that such a thing would never exist. Why did you have to die first?" Brenner sobbed and covered his face with his hands in shame. "I wanted to be the one that died first. I'm not strong enough."

"I know, love. I'm so sorry." Lily looked sad but didn't join her husband in tears. "Brenner, whenever you want to remember with me, just hold my hands and we can go back."

They sat silently, staring into each other's eyes until suddenly, Lily shot a sharp glance at the edge of the clearing on Brenner's right. The waxy thicket of mountain laurel Brenner had traversed on his way to the clearing was rippling with movement. Several birds flew from nests into the sky.

"Is someone with you?!" Lily asked, her voice changed from sweet and innocent to accusatory. To Brenner's surprise she now seemed to be glaring at him.

"I—uhm, yeah, remember my note to you? I made a friend. I thought you would be happy for me."

"Oh—well, of course I'm happy for you." Lily looked nervous and forcibly changed her tone to something feigning compassion once more, her annoyance thinly veiled. "It's just… other people shouldn't see me, baby. They won't understand. He will come between us, Brenner."

"Won't you come with us?" Brenner asked, remembering his journey on the trail, one whose purpose he had now forgotten entirely.

"You're still going with him? Stay with me, Brenner!" Lily pleaded, desperately.

Just then, Rami stumbled through the opening in the trail, wiping his eyes to help them adjust and focus on the clearing. Before Brenner could muster a response, Lily evaporated, like morning mist from atop a stream, reaching tendrilled fingers skyward to join the moisture suspended in clouds somewhere high above. The silence was whisked away with what remained of his wife in a cool breeze.

"What are you doing out here?" Rami asked, once he noticed Brenner sitting against the large stone. "This place feels off—unnatural." He shuddered as he looked around the clearing.

"I couldn't sleep, so I wanted to explore the area around camp," Brenner lied, still looking at an undefinable point in the air in front of him that was seconds before occupied by the wife he never thought he would see again.

Rami raised his eyebrows and searched Brenner's face. "Fair enough," he finally said. "You ready to head towards Franklin?"

Remembering their plans for the day, but still somewhat mesmerized by the previous few minutes—or hours, Brenner responded, "Yeah, but I need to pack up camp." On cue, Sam exploded from the opening and ran to her owner, wagged her tail, and then turned back towards the opening, beckoning Brenner to follow.

"Already done, brother."

Chapter 11

"I was looking at the map and noticed right before the Rock gap shelter there is a side trail that leads to Laurel Branch," Rami said, a few hours later as the sun rose higher in the sky.

"Oh yeah?" Brenner responded, half listening, his mind still on Lily. He sipped the remainder of the dark, rich coffee Rami had brewed for them that morning. *Stay with me, Brenner.*

Rami stopped and turned to look at his friend. "Yeah. Hey, Brenner, what's going on man? You haven't said a word this morning. Are you okay? I didn't mean to bring all that up about Lily. Is that what's on your mind?"

Brenner's stomach lurched at her name. He had the feeling that each step along the trail was stripping away any remaining chance of seeing his wife again. And yet, he couldn't stay where he'd been. "No," he lied, "I'm just tired, I think. There was either a squirrel or a raccoon doing their best bear impression last night while I was trying to fall asleep."

"Okay man, if you say so." Rami turned and continued

walking, now at a steady incline towards another false ridge. Neither of them spoke for several minutes, but rather panted and shed sweat in the intense morning rays that increased the effort of their climb. Their backs steamed as they trudged forward. Even Sam seemed exhausted. When the trail flattened, Rami and Brenner paused with hands on knees to catch their breath. "Anyway, what I was going to say was Laurel Branch looks to be a decent tributary of the Nantahala."

Brenner's eyes lit up and he turned toward Rami. Only one thing would help him forget his wife, in both this current moment and when she was still living. "Maybe it's big enough—"

"—big enough to hold fish. Exactly, my friend."

"Well, hell Rami. Why didn't you just say so?" Brenner smiled and immediately started hiking forward with Sam, leading for the first time that day.

"Uh huh, that's what I thought." Rami laughed.

Mid-afternoon, the three companions sat on a log, covered in Turkey Tails, that lay decaying on the side of the trail. They were at the intersection of the Appalachian Trail and Timber Ridge Trail. Sam lay draped over the log, two legs hanging from each side, with her head resting on Brenner's lap, hoping by some miracle he would drop a piece of jerky. Brenner forgot about food when fishing, so he insisted upon eating before hiking to the river, to not deprive his body of the energy he continued to so readily burn while hiking.

"Can I ask you something?" Rami interrupted the sound of chewing and sent the squirrels that rustled ahead on the trail quickly up into the trees.

"Sure."

"Do you believe in ghosts?"

Brenner sat motionless. A curious question, given the timing. "I don't know. Maybe." He waited for a response from Rami but realized he hadn't produced an adequate answer, and no response came. "I mean, I think I do—now at least."

"Why now and not before?" Rami stopped eating and looked at Brenner.

"I don't know, Rami. Why are you asking?" He grew annoyed at this inquisition. "Do you believe in ghosts?"

"Absolutely not," Rami said tersely.

"How can you be so sure?"

"Because there is nothing in the Bible about ghosts. Despite all the topics left up to interpretation, the Bible is crystal clear on what happens to souls when the body passes."

"Then what about all the haunted places in the world? The shows on T.V., the ghost tours, mediums, Ouija boards, any of that?" Brenner asked.

"I believe in spirits, but I don't think they're no ghosts, Brenner. I believe in angels and demons. I think it's incredibly dangerous to believe in ghosts and to let your mind sit on those things."

The conversation made Brenner uneasy, and it felt like some sort of accusation. He became defensive, like a child answering to an overbearing parent. "Okay, well we can all believe what we want, can't we?"

"I just think we have to be careful, that's all." Rami frowned, seeing Brenner's mood had soured.

"I'm finished eating," Brenner finally responded. "Let's go catch some fish."

***

The trail meandered along the sloping, descending ridge steadily until at last, the sound of crashing water cascaded out of suspension in the air and poured into the ears of the travelers, awakening their souls, tired from a day of hiking. Brenner began jogging, neck craned, gaze peering through the foliage. The sound of the waterfall grew louder, and he turned off the trail into the thick of the woods. Sam and Rami followed until they finally exited the brush and stumbled upon a beautiful pool and tail out at the base of a ten-foot tall, three-tiered rock face, over which flowed Laurel Branch. The narrow creek was flattened into a thin sheet as it coursed the subsequent rocks and ultimately dumped into the pool, likely the deepest part of the creek for miles.

The average fisherman would pass on fishing something so small, but this was Brenner's bread and butter. Had someone challenged him, he would have bet his life savings on the fact that just under the surface of the water a dozen colorful brook trout would be darting back and forth, consuming whatever insects the creek sent over the falls into their feeding zone. Moreover, these fish would not be wary of flies, line, or hooks, as they were as virgin as the day they emerged as fry. "Tie on anything," he told Rami when they started casting.

The dozen fish Brenner had hoped for were reduced to a mere two apiece, strikingly beautiful, as always. Brenner and Rami continued casting long after they knew all the fish were either caught or spooked, fly line hissing through the air in big loops, gently dropping little feathered flies on the surface of the water. At one point Rami looked at Brenner after the latter had a particularly good cast that put his fly along the right bank. Rami then cast to almost the same spot, only closer to the bank.

Suddenly, casting had turned into a competition. Brenner focused his next cast towards the left bank, fly lazily landing a foot from the rooted soil that gently sloped into the water. Rami followed with yet another superior cast, his fly landing six inches closer to the bank. Brenner chuckled to himself and picked up the line to cast again. This time he let too much line fly forward and his little mayfly imitation wrapped itself around a rhododendron branch. He tried once to pull it free. When the fly didn't budge, he glanced at Rami and closed his eyes in defeat. Rami smiled.

Brenner waded through the knee-deep water to the bank fifteen yards away and climbed out of the water to grab his fly. He squinted as he tried to concentrate on the thin, clear tippet that was, despite barely contacting the meandering branch, wrapped in a tangled web. Brenner grumbled to himself, frustrated by the knotted line, and slightly embarrassed that Rami had just won their spontaneous casting competition. It seemed that Rami was one of those people that just easily picked up on things. And yet, there was something more about Rami, that Brenner couldn't put his finger on—something odd, even.

Brenner was pulled from his thoughts as a whispering sound came through the forest to his left, interrupting his focus on the knotted mess. He jolted and tried to peer through the interwoven branches of creek-side foliage, suddenly aware of his breathing. He looked back to see if the sound had come from Rami or Sam, who both now had disappeared from the pool.

"Brenner..."

"Lily?" Brenner knew the voice and left his fly dangling from the waxy leaves, taking several hopeful steps in the direction of the call. "Lily, where are you?"

"I'm right here, baby. Come find me." The words reverberated in the air, as if they were spoken from a parallel dimension of space and time, echoing softly with the melody of sweet, haunted longing.

Brenner's pace picked up and he briskly walked away from the water through the heart of the woods, forgetting about Rami and his dog. The gentle afternoon breeze birthed an enormous gust that shook the canopy violently and drowned out the sound of the creek. Brenner continued in the direction of the voice.

"You're almost there," Lily said, after the young vet had been walking for around five minutes.

"Are you here, Lily? I'm coming for you." Brenner's heart raced. He acutely felt two strong and opposite emotions. A sense of fearful foreboding clawed at his mind, one that showed him the events of the preceding months—the funeral they had held for Lily, his attempts at moving on, the decision to hike the Appalachian Trail, the interactions with Lily the last few days… However, the other emotion he felt was in his heart and not his mind. Love. Brenner felt a desperate desire to cling to any memory of his wife, his soulmate. The heart wants what the heart wants, and love supersedes all other emotions, good and bad, for better or for worse. Thus, he pressed forward, ignoring the reservation.

He ducked under a low-hanging branch and finally left the stand of rhododendron behind, finding himself now amid a boulder field, large ancient rocks standing like stone giants, cast down the mountainside at some distant point in the past. He weaved his way through them, hoping to see his wife around every corner. Worried he might have started walking in the wrong direction, Brenner decided to sit for a minute in silence and listen. Wanting a better vantage point, he hoisted himself up onto a flat stony ledge that extended from one of the larger boulders. He thought of Sam, which caused his stomach to churn, but then quickly told himself that Rami was certainly with her. He sat quietly for fifteen minutes, straining to hear anything unnatural in the forest, but the sounds that found their way into his ears were ones expected for this setting.

Brenner grew impatient and stood. "Lily!" he shouted, causing several birds to fly out of a nearby oak. Nothing. "Lily, where are you?!" His voice was strained and desperate, sad even. He collapsed back onto the stone and whimpered, several tears finding their way to his cheeks. "What the hell am I doing? Goddamnit!" He slammed his fist, which was grasping a smaller rock, onto the stone surface he was sitting upon. At that moment, something stirred closely behind him. He moved to the side to reveal he had been sitting in front of a crevice in the rock. As he moved away from the crevice, his eyes were drawn by a large, dark shape draped across the stone on the opposite side of the ledge. *Shit.*

Immediately a loud rhythmic buzzing started, and Brenner watched as the shape curled up into a series of concentric circles. The snake was dark brown with copper bands wrapped around its five-inch-thick body. Brenner slowly backed away, as it continued rattling. At the same time, two more Timber rattlesnakes emerged from the crevice he had rested against just moments before. The first snake lashed out with a warning strike, hissing as its head exploded forward towards Brenner. He was running out of room to back away, and the two snakes emerging from their den had started moving towards him and were taking up offensive positions.

The route he had taken to pull himself up on the ledge was inaccessible now, so Brenner started looking for a soft spot on the ground to land. In a panic, Brenner threw himself from the large boulder and came crashing down on the ground, allowing his shoulder to take the brunt of the fall as he rolled to a stop, inches from a large maple tree. When he lifted his head, he shouted and rolled backwards, as he found himself face to face with a fourth and final rattlesnake, one that he had nearly landed on. The snake reacted immediately to nearly being crushed and lashed out with the speed of a hummingbird's wingbeat, striking Brenner on his hand, one he had thrown up in defense to protect his face.

"Fuck!" Brenner cried, finally able to stand and sprint away from the apparent snake nest. His hand hurt, but the strike had been quick. He ignored the pain and forgot his wife, wanting only to be back with Rami and Sam. He was already hoping and pleading that it was a dry bite, one meant to ward off predators, and not a true envenomation. From taking several classes on snakes in veterinary school, he was well aware of the potent neurotoxin harbored in the venom glands of Timber, or "Canebrake", rattlesnakes. The toxin was capable of binding neuromuscular receptors on the diaphragm, causing diaphragmatic paralysis and ultimately suffocation. *Please, please, please be a dry bite.* Brenner looked up towards Heaven, or at least where he supposed it would be, if it existed.

Leaving a trail of broken leaves and snapped branches in his wake, he crashed through the thicket of waxy foliage and twisted wood, moving in the direction he hoped would lead him back to the waterfall. He kept the bitten hand raised above his head as best he could, fixated onto each breath—measuring its strength and volume against every preceding one.

He wasn't just waiting for the one that would come up short. He was anticipating it—the one that would be fractured, labored, and, perhaps, final.

His temples throbbed in sync with his racing heart. Sweat, which should have felt warm, clung to his skin with a clammy chill. With every frantic stride, he drove another nail into his coffin. *I could die.*

So distracted was Brenner by his fatalistic mindset, he did not register the end of the woods, and more importantly, the bank of the pool below the waterfall. His startled attempt to check his momentum came too late and Brenner went sliding into the waist-deep water with all the grace of a shot duck. This certainly did not help his nerves, and he splashed around hysterically until he found his footing, realizing the pool was quite shallow.

He stood up abruptly to find a shape moving quickly toward him, as his eyes shed remnants of the creek and attempted to focus. Arms thrown in front of him, Brenner braced for contact, unsure whether he was being haunted or hunted. His life was now a combination of heart-wrenching teases intermixed with sheer horror. Would his outstretched hands meet a charging bear or perhaps the memory of his wife? Somehow that possibility felt no less terrifying. In the split second between his rising and drying his eyes, the object reached him, and they went crashing back into the water, together. Sam.

"Samantha!" he shouted, as his dog jumped up and down over him in the water, causing Brenner to momentarily forget the preceding events. He even smiled.

"Where did you go?" a familiar voice asked.

"Rami?" Brenner looked up at the bank. "I—Where did *you* go? I went to look for you." He hadn't, but Rami had left the waterfall immediately before Brenner was called into the woods so it sounded plausible.

"I didn't go anywhere. We've been waiting for you to come back." Rami cocked his head to the side and studied Brenner.

"No, you and Sam left the pool before I did."

"We did not. I called your name as you walked away from us. I asked you where you were going. Sam even followed you for a few minutes before running back to me. Brenner, where did you go?"

"You weren't there…" Brenner mumbled, more to himself than to Rami. He tried to remember the moment he left the waterfall, but the memory evaded him, and his mind felt heavy. A sharp pain from his left hand pulled him back into the present moment and the panic awoke once more. "Rami! I was bit! I was bit by a—a rattlesnake." He scrambled towards his friend, collapsing into his arms when he reached the bank. Emotions, memories, and fear bubbled over, and Brenner wept.

"Hold on. It's going to be okay. Let me look at it." Rami cupped the back of Brenner's neck as he spoke, trying to calm him down.

Brenner stepped back and extended his hand. As he did, both he and Rami stared in silent awe. Brenner's hand hovered in the air, at waist level, parallel to the ground below. The contrast with the richly dark soil threw each extended finger into sharp relief. Brenner gestured with his other hand to show Rami the bite, but there was nothing there. Despite his finger still throbbing with pain, the skin was smooth and unpunctured. Brenner realized, as he was pointing to a nonexistent snake bite, that he was in fact pointing to the base of his left ring finger.

"That's peculiar," Rami whispered, barely audible. He then turned and stared at Brenner, something that made the latter feel his soul was being searched, rendering him uncomfortable enough to turn and look away into the forest.

"I swear it was there—on that finger! I don't know what's going on."

"How are you feeling?" Rami asked, as he examined Brenner's hand more closely.

"I don't know. I think I'm going crazy, Rami. What do you think?" Brenner felt his heart slow, but his mind continued to race. "It still hurts," he added.

"I don't know what to think. I believe you—I really do. I'm

not sure if you are just experiencing trauma, lingering effects of mushrooms, or a downright haunting. Either way, I think it's about time we got to Franklin." Rami kept caring eye contact with Brenner as he spoke and then gently squeezed his shoulders.

"It feels like it might be all three," Brenner responded as he felt Sam's wet tongue lick his arm.

As they hiked away from the fishing hole, Brenner's mind moved past the terror of respiratory paralysis and settled itself firmly on Lily, and more specifically how the phantom snake bite could be related. *Could it really be her?* As he rubbed the pain from his finger, he also pondered the location of the bite. *What does it mean?*

During the last few months, since Lily's passing, leading up to the trip, something horrible had started happening to Brenner—something that made him loathe himself. Every once and a while, when he thought of his wife, her face began to elude him. Obviously when he looked at pictures, he knew what she looked like. But for some reason, when he just thought about her, he struggled to imagine the shape of her nose, the fullness of her eyebrows, the size of her ears. It was the details… He was starting to forget. He didn't want to forget. He *couldn't* forget, or else he feared he would go crazy. He'd do anything to see her face again.

Chapter 12

Later that night as his finger finally stopped throbbing, Brenner drifted into a deep sleep, mind stripped of any remaining energy or desire to stay awake. They had not made it quite to Highway 64 with the events of that afternoon, instead setting up camp just past where they fished.

When Brenner's eyes closed to the cool Appalachian night, they opened to the comfort of his bedroom back home. He stretched his legs and enjoyed the softness of the sheets. When he looked to his right, Lily was lying on her side, facing him, and smiled.

"Hey sweetie," she said tenderly. "I sure do love you."

Brenner tried to shake the cloudiness from his mind, not remembering how he got there. "I love you too, babe. How long have you been awake?"

"Not long. I can't fall back asleep, though, and I wanted to watch you sleep."

"Do you want to talk?"

"I would love that." She scooted closer to him and draped her arm around his neck, wiggling her body next to his.

"What's on your mind, Lil?"

"I just miss the days when it was just us."

Oh boy, Brenner thought, realizing he was in for more than just "pillow-talk". "What do you mean, sweetheart? It is just us." He dramatically looked around the room to indicate no one was with them.

"Oh, don't be silly. I know it's just us in here. I just mean… I guess… I miss the days when we spent all day and every day together. You know? The beginning."

"Well, what do you want me to do? Quit my job?" Brenner laughed.

"That would be a start!" Lily laughed too.

"Well, yesterday we went to…" Brenner's voice trailed off as he realized he had no recollection of the preceding day's event. He squinted hard and tried to concentrate.

"Yesterday, you followed my voice into the woods, but then never found me."

Brenner's blood turned to ice as he watched Lily's mouth move. "I'm dreaming."

"Well, of course you're dreaming, Brenner! You're peacefully sleeping in the woods. And may I add, you look handsome as ever, though somewhat unwashed."

Brenner considered the possibility that the spirit of Lily was in his tent, watching him sleep.

"Lily, you died."

"But yet here I am. I want it to just be us again."

"I tried to find you. You weren't there. All I found was a rattlesnake nest."

"It's because we weren't going to be alone."

"What do you mean?"

"Your… friend."

"Rami?"

"That one. I don't want to be around him. It's not good for him to see me."

"Lily, I don't want to hike alone, and Rami is my friend. I can't just leave him."

"So, you're choosing someone you just met over your wife."

"Lily, you DIED!"

"I'm right here, honey."

Lily put her hand on Brenner's arm and when she did a burst of energy ran through his body, sending tendrils of warmth and desire coursing through his entire being, physical and spiritual. Brenner jolted awake, sitting up so suddenly that Sam flinched before crawling to his side to lick his face.

"Nice. Really nice." He wiped her saliva from his cheek. "Ugh," he groaned and thought about Lily's demand. On the one hand, he had grown close to Rami the last few days, closer than he'd thought possible. He had comforted him at times when Brenner needed it most. The mushroom trip, the snake bite. Beyond that, Brenner was frankly scared to be alone, unsure he could trust his mind or his body on the trail ahead. However, on the other hand, Lily was his wife. *Was. Was. Was.*

His mind continued trying to find every reason to stay with Rami, like bullet points, logical. That position seemed to require effort and reasoning. The default of Brenner's mind was terrifying but required no effort. In fact, when Brenner tried to let his mind be still, it found its way back to one thing. He wanted to be with Lily. He'd gone on this journey to heal, but all along healing had seemed to be impossible without closure. The trip so far had given him the opposite. The presence of Lily's spirit meant one of two things. Either Brenner would find closure, or he would somehow find a way to be with her once again. He didn't know how such a thing could be possible, but merely days before he'd been certain it was impossible to ever even see her again. Maybe there was a way.

I know what I have to do.

The night was quiet, the hour somewhere between the eerie last calls of nocturnal creatures and the awakening calls of the day walkers. The witching hour.

Determined to be sensible, if only to prove to himself this was a plan and not a fit of madness, Brenner turned on his headlamp, confirming it had not, for some reason, run out of charge. *Would a madman check his equipment?* He cupped the light in his hand, and it shone soft red through the blood-filled capillaries of his fingers. Three out of four small bars lit up on the side.

"Okay, Sam. We have to be quiet." The dog cocked her head and let out a soft whimper. "No, Sam. *Shhh!*" He first deflated his sleeping pad and stowed it in a side pocket of his backpack.

Next, Brenner rolled and stuffed his sleeping bag. The dirty clothes from the day before were still quite damp from his unintended swim near the waterfall and he zipped them into a waterproof front pocket, to not dirty the few remaining clean clothes in the bag. One by one, the remainder of his possessions were cleared from the tent and neatly put away. He spent the better part of a minute slowly unzipping the door of his tent, one tiny prong at a time, pausing when it made any noise louder than a whisper.

When the door was finally agape and he poked his head into the cool air, he heard the gentle snoring of Rami and frowned, feeling sad that he was leaving his companion, though not enough to stay. He'd come out here to get his head right alone, hadn't he? And it felt right.

He quickly tethered Sam to the nearest tree and leaned close to her ear. "Stay." The hound started shaking her hind end and lifted her head back to bark. "No, Sam! Stay!" His quieted voice strained as he struggled to convey the importance of his command without waking Rami. Sam dropped her head and sighed.

The stakes were easy enough to pull and Brenner dropped them into a small bag. He then disconnected the two long, intersecting poles from the corners of the tent. Once the rain fly was folded neatly, Brenner rolled the loose tent up around the rain fly until it was compressed enough to be placed with the poles back into its sack. He strapped the tent to his backpack and went to free his dog from the tree. She lifted her front feet off the ground repeatedly in excitement as he separated leash and pine.

Walking quietly, taking care not to step on loose foliage, Brenner walked to the trail. Before turning northward, the young veterinarian turned and whispered into the night, in the direction of Rami's tent, "Goodbye. Thanks for everything." As the words left his mouth, he heard a loud yawn and a rustling of nylon. *Shit!* Without waiting another moment, Brenner put the campsite behind him and hurried quietly up the Appalachian Trail, alone but for his four-legged companion, who seemed unbothered by the early hour of their exodus.

What life was Brenner now living? After an hour of hiking with the headlamp, he now walked in silent darkness as the moon and early haze of dawn illuminated enough of the trail to guide his steps. The life he had left behind in Greenville—the job, the patients, the coworkers, even the mourning—slowly slipped away from his increasingly fragile grasp of reality. He found himself progressing in a trance-like state towards an unknown purpose, but one he knew to involve Lily. Everything his rational mind once clung to as substrate was sinking into the quicksand of either disillusioned hope, or perhaps hopelessness. Did having seen Lily make him happier or was it contributing to a deep-seated depression where she existed just beyond his reach, somewhere in the ethereal plane between living and dead?

Brenner forwent rationalism and even self-preservation as he left Rami behind. Whether it was a never-ending waking dream or more real than the life he'd left behind, he was determined to see it through. At least he had Samantha and wasn't truly alone. His dog gave him significant comfort and peace of mind. She was a tangible lifeline to reality, something—someone—he could cling to when the rest of the world spun around him.

While Brenner pondered metaphysics, she was chasing an early-rising chipmunk back up a tree to his right. She let out a loud, frustrated bay, causing several birds to scatter from the canopy overhead. Far enough from anyone who would care, Brenner let her bark to her heart's content. When he failed to acknowledge her signaling towards the chipmunk, she lost interest and bounded forward. He was the tortoise, she the hare. They continued moving forward at very different paces for another hour, stopping only to watch the new day's sun bleed the horizon, causing it to leak soft orange and blue.

He'd done as Lily asked but now there was no sign of her. Without guidance he supposed his plan remained the same. He would head off the trail long enough to restock and then continue on. Maybe getting back to civilization would break Lily's spell and he'd be able to decide if that was the right thing to do. He was torn, unsure breaking the spell was even what he wanted, but his supplies were dwindling.

Brenner had never been to Franklin before and didn't know much about it, beyond the basics he'd gleaned from a quick look at a map he found online. He knew the outfitting store, which claimed to be stocked with the most delicious, gourmet freeze-dried meals, was on W Main Street. That took care of the resupplying; that was his priority. Beyond that he had focused his search on Main Street for two other necessities: a fly shop and a bar.

Although he was eager to resume his search for Lily, Brenner convinced himself that a night off the trail was what he needed. A night to clear his head and reassess. A night to grab a beer—or six. He had become accustomed to drinking his sorrow away. He also, irrationally, reckoned that alcohol might give him a little mental clarity and help him deconstruct the dam he had built in his mind against the stream of raw, unpolished consciousness.

Since he planned to indulge, Brenner thought his best plan would be to stay a night in the motel just down the road from the bar, which was just down the road from the fly shop, which was just down the road from the outfitter, which was just down the road from everything else in downtown Franklin according to the map.

Brenner was pulled from his thoughts when Sam let out a loud, sustained howl. She was barking at cars. "We made it to the road, ole gal." He smiled as he clipped the leash to her harness. "Now all that's left to do is get a ride." She started wagging her tail. "Ride" just so happened to be one of her favorite words.

The two stood side by side on a small gravel pull off as Brenner began the process of finding a shuttle—a process that required a cell phone. Brenner tried to remember the name of the shuttle company he had found for Franklin as he pressed the button to turn on his phone, which was left off to conserve battery life. The screen remained black. Thinking he pressed the wrong button, he tried again. Nothing.

"DAMN IT!" he shouted, kicking the closest rock he could find. Samantha watched the rock bounce down the highway and then looked back up at her owner. "Well, I suppose hitchhiking it is. Look pretty, Sam, and..." He paused for effect. She patiently waited. "I don't want to hear another goddamn bark." She wiggled her hips back and forth with excitement at such a personal address, not knowing what he had said. Then she barked.

Now, the two stood side by side once again—this time, just off the parking lot, near the not-so-busy highway. Brenner's thumb and Sam's tail stood equally erect, both ready to flag down a stranger, gamble on their goodwill, and hope they'd be dropped off on W Main Street—or at least close enough to walk.

He chuckled at the thought of Lily hitchhiking, knowing she wouldn't be caught dead trusting a stranger. She'd lose her mind if she knew he was doing this with Sam.

But then the chuckle faded.

A thought crept in, chilling in its possibility—what if she already knew?

He spun around, scanning the gaps between the trees, half-expecting to see her standing there.

I need to think about something else.

As if on cue, Brenner's stomach let out a long, melodious—symphonic, even—growl that continued for so long Sam looked at his midsection and turned her head to the side. "Dang, I'm kind of hungry, girl." With the use of another one of her favorite words so soon after the first, Sam was unable to contain herself and ignored the command from her dad and began howling. Brenner ignored his dog and imagined what he might eat for dinner at the bar. Perhaps a hamburger. Or tacos? No… chicken wings. His mouth watered at the thought of his first real food in several days. At first, he pictured wings dripping with classic buffalo sauce, buttery and wet. A warm, almost cozy burn on his lips, quenchable only by a smothering of ranch or blue cheese—or both. But garlic parmesan, even teriyaki was entrancing. *I'll get all of them.*

"Hey! Flames!" Brenner was so deep in his subconscious wonderland of fried chicken wings that he did not immediately register the vehicle that had stopped in front of him and the howling hound. He flinched as his mind was pulled back into the present moment and blinked hard two or three times.

"Sticks?"

"You do remember me, dude!" Sticks beamed. "And if it isn't old…" He paused and looked back and forth from Sam to Brenner, obviously waiting for some help.

"Samantha," Brenner mumbled, as he debated whether he

should forgo his resupply to avoid continuing talking to this man he thought one hair shy of clinically insane.

***

Brenner didn't know it, but Sticks, for all his quirks and oddities, had turned out much better than most who started with the deck of cards he was dealt with as a child. He couldn't remember a time when his father wasn't drunk, even when he was a small boy. He lied to his friends—if you could call them that—at school, saying his dad was "upper management", though he didn't know exactly what that meant. They laughed and made drinking gestures to him, turning their hands up in front of their faces to mimic upturned bottles, or walking in exaggerated zigzags on the playground. Alan—his real name—was strong and never cried. At least, that is, he never cried in front of them.

By the time Alan made it to high school, his mother, often covered in bruises or scrapes that were ignored by all, began to partake in the other demon of Southern Appalachia—methamphetamine. She haunted the halls of their trailer every night, wandering to and fro, always seeming to be looking for something.

Alan saved every penny he made from his job at the video store, knowing each one put him a step closer to moving out of hell. Long hours cut into study time and Alan's grades continued in a downward slide. When finally, he picked up shop to say goodbye to the single-wide and stumbling idiots, his grades had fallen enough to make him realize college would never happen.

Thus, Alan followed the path of many socially awkward high school rejects and joined a metal band named "Void Attics". The name "Void Addicts", and with it the fringy definition "addicted to the nothingness", was already taken and the band members found the substitute funny enough to keep it. Not long afterward strumming power chords in dropped D tuning began to lose its novelty and the band members let Alan in on a secret: they were not in fact addicted to the nothingness. They were addicted to heroin. Alan held out for months, occasionally looking at pictures of his pre-drug mother as motivation. Finally, however, Alan gave in and began using.

Well, one thing led to another as he accelerated down the same dark road as the two people responsible for his procreation and Alan eventually found himself in jail at the ripe age of eighteen years old, right around the time the bullies from his youth were getting college invitations from Appalachian State, Clemson, and Western North Carolina. Fortunately, only charged with possession of marijuana, Alan spent no more than a few nights in jail with court-ordered community service.

The troubled adolescent man cursed the world and everything in it as he walked up and down the Blue Ridge Parkway with the pointed stick, neatly making piles of beer cans, empty chips bags, and Styrofoam cups. On the fifth day of clean-up, he was laughed at by a white-collar prick and his family driving along the parkway in a Land Rover, windows down to make sure he heard them. Alan kicked a beer can down off the road and into the woods. Feeling guilty, he walked down the embankment to retrieve his own piece of litter.

He pushed apart a few branches of rich green firs to find the can and suddenly stopped in his tracks, captivated by the color and texture of the trees. *Why am I cursing the world?* he thought. *It's the people that need cursing. My parents, my teachers, my so-called friends. The world is the only thing that's never hurt me.* He sat down beside the creek that ran along the road, hidden by the firs, and cried.

From that day forward, Alan was granola and green. His entire life turned around. He passed his GED, quit using heroin, dropped out of the band, and started working at the local outfitter store in Franklin, one town over from his hometown. He grew to love people again, but only through the help of nature. His soul and his mind healed more each day he breathed the fresh air of the mountains. He also decided he would only take a drug if it grew naturally from the ground. Hence, the mushrooms.

He had been ripening in his new niche for several years before happening upon Brenner on the trail. Socially awkward?

Yes. Overwhelming? Yes. Maybe even full-blown weird? Yep. But given his starting point, Sticks had done alright with his life.

***

Of course, Brenner knew none of this and still thought Sticks was weird enough to avoid. But it wasn't like he had a lot of options, and he didn't like the idea of walking along the shoulder all the way to town.

"Let me help you with your pack, dude. I know those things are quite the burden to bear at this point in your journey!" Before Brenner could react, Sticks had jumped out of the car and was pulling Brenner's pack off. "Franklin, am I right?!"

There was no use in arguing and he wasn't likely to have much luck finding another ride with a dead phone. He also knew Sticks wouldn't charge him for the shuttle. Sam eagerly hopped into the back seat and wagged her tail. She liked Sticks and his almost dog-like energy. Brenner ignored the strange blue stains on the seat as he climbed in through the passenger door. Given how filthy he was at this point it probably didn't matter. "Thanks for the ride, Sticks. My phone died and I'd have been waiting for a while if you hadn't shown up."

"Brother, don't even mention it. I had a suspicion that our paths might cross again. In fact, I prayed for it."

Brenner let out a subtle, forced chuckle. "So, a man of God, are we?"

"God, gods, mother nature, you name it dude. I prayed to whatever's in control, and here we are. He, she, or it listened."

"Indeed, they did."

Sticks reached for the dial and turned on the radio. "Do you like rock?"

"Uhm, yeah, as much as the next guy, I suppose."

"Who?

"Who what?"

"You like it as much as who?"

"The next guy."

"The next guy?"

"Yeah, the next guy." Brenner's blood pressure started to rise.

"Who's that?"

"It's an expression."

"I've never heard it."

"It means—you know what? Never mind. It doesn't matter." He looked at Sticks, who was nodding his head to some unknown beat, his long hair blowing in the mountain air pouring in through his open window. "How about that rock?"

"Where?!" Sticks stuck his head out of the window and looked at the side of the road, eyes searching the edge of the woods. He didn't notice the pickup truck heading towards them and swerved slightly into the oncoming lane.

"Jesus Christ!" Brenner shouted, causing Sticks to veer sharply back into the correct lane. Sam fell over in the back seat.

"Ah, it seems that you, Flames, are the man of God! Jesus Christ, indeed."

"What were you doing?" Brenner shrieked.

"I was looking for the rock!"

"Ugh!" Brenner moaned—accidentally aloud.

He stared out the window, turning this moment over in his mind, trying to place it within the bigger picture of his life. Sticks felt more like a cartoon character than a real person. As he replayed their conversation, he let himself smile. Lately, life had been drained of humor, every moment weighted with seriousness and sorrow. Maybe it was good to find a little levity—even if it came in the form of a hitched ride with a man who called himself Sticks.

"Where to, compadre?" the latter asked from the driver's seat after finding a suitable song.

"Franklin Outdoors. I need to restock."

"Eureka! What a coincidence! Yours truly happens to be under the employment of the aforementioned 'Franklin Outdoors'."

"Of course you are," Brenner said under his breath.

"What was that?"

"Oh, I asked 'About how far?' And no kidding? That's awesome! Maybe you could help me pick some things out." The words kind of just fell out of Brenner's mouth.

"The honor would be mine."

Twenty minutes later, after fist bumping every coworker in the building, Sticks pointed to several freeze-dried meals, also known as MREs. "You don't want that one, dude." He gestured towards the "Chili Mac". "I ate that when I was camping last summer in Georgia, and it ran through me like my mouth was connected to my caboose with a straight pipe. And a greased one at that. I'm telling you; I could crap through a screen door." He soberly shook his head side to side and sighed, like he was remembering a lost loved one.

Brenner laughed. "Sticks, has anyone ever told you that you're kind of crazy?"

"Brother, I hear it at least once before second breakfast every day."

"Ah, a Lord of the Rings fan?"

"My dog's name is Tom Bombadil, so I'd say…" Sticks squinted and looked towards the ceiling, "…Yes! I think I'd say I'm a bit of a Lord of the Rings fan." He then bellowed laughter, as if the question was ridiculous.

"You want to get a beer after this?" Brenner asked, now finding at least one thing they had in common. He was starting to kind of like Sticks.

Chapter 13

"Wait, brother… HOW many mushrooms did you eat?" Sticks asked, leaving his mouth agape. The pair sat at a bar three doors down from the outdoors store and about six doors down from the motel at which Brenner had booked a room for the night.

"Half of them."

"No wonder you tripped, dude! The only time I ate that many cubes was when I was trying to heal from some *heavy, heavy* juju, and I swear my mind left my body. I remember looking down at myself for what seemed like a lifetime, begging myself to wake up or vomit out the shrooms. I think it only helped me heal because when I came to, I wasn't even the same person anymore."

"Well, Sticks, I sure wish you had told me that on the front end."

"To be honest, man," Sticks frowned, "I kind of thought I'd scared you away. You seemed eager to get out of there. I have that effect on people sometimes."

Brenner's heart sank. "I'm sorry, it wasn't you. I promise. I'll be honest with you too. I'm *currently* trying to heal from some pretty heavy shit. And frankly, I'm not sure if I'm healing or just going crazy at this point."

"You, uh, want to talk about it?" Sticks asked softly.

"It's just that…" Brenner trailed off. "I just lost…" Silence occupied the space between them for several seconds. "My wife died, Sticks. She died a few weeks ago—months ago, shit I don't even know. Every day feels like an eternity. I don't even know what day it is anymore. I told myself, 'Just take it one day at a time, Bren', but it's hard to do that when I can't remember when one day ends and the next starts." Sticks looked down at the bar, clearly listening but also giving Brenner space to tell his story the way he needed to.

"She drowned in a river in Charleston. She went swimming after dark. She'd been drinking. We had a fight the day before she died, and I cannot get past the what ifs. What if I'd gone with her? What if I'd said the thing that would have made her come with me instead? What if I could just take back the shit I said?

"That's why I'm out here. I thought maybe, if I could get away from the rest of the world, and only have to think about hiking and camping, maybe nature would heal me, maybe I could finally get past what if." Brenner wiped his eyes with the back of his arm.

Sticks looked up from the bar and into Brenner's eyes, showing Brenner that he too had started crying. With wet lines running down his face, Sticks embraced Brenner in a hug and told him, "You're gonna to be okay, brother. Everything's going to be alright. Time heals all. Believe me when I say that because I've been there, too. Time heals all wounds."

"Thanks, Sticks."

"That's one of the saddest things I've heard. I'm so sorry that happened to you. Bad things never happen to bad people, so you must be a good person."

"There's something else."

Sticks' eyes focused on Brenner's face, ready for whatever he had to say, as he took another sip of his India Pale Ale.

"I've seen her since she died. I've seen her in the mountains. The first time was when I ate all those mushrooms. I thought I was being haunted by something, but it was—"

"You can't trust a trip, man."

"No, but it's happened every day since then. She approached me in a dream and told me to come find her in the woods, so I did. She's out there. I saw her with my own eyes. I touched her and she showed me old memories."

Sticks looked concerned, scared even. "Listen, dude, I don't know what it is you saw, but I doubt it's your wife. I can't imagine going through what you've been through, and I know your heart probably aches for her, but dead people don't stick around. If there is no Heaven, people just die. If there is a Heaven, they go straight there. Why would they stick around?"

Brenner set down his empty glass bottle and pensively twisted it in circles in front of him. "I don't know why, or how, but I know I saw her."

"I've had wicked hallucinations before, Flames. I mean *wicked.* I once hallucinated that I was riding a horse—Shadowfax, actually. I rode him for hours. My thighs even felt sore afterward, man! It was wild."

"I don't think I'm hallucinating, and I only actually tripped that one time."

"I dunno. Maybe you should see a doctor."

"Maybe." Brenner knew he shouldn't have told Sticks about Lily. He knew he wouldn't believe him, but then again, who would? What sane person would ever believe him? Maybe he should just head home. He could find a ride back to his 4Runner and leave this all behind. It was the sane thing to do.

He couldn't live in the woods forever. He didn't know if she would come back with him. Even if she did, he would have to keep her a secret, partly because she seemed to not want to be discovered and because people would count him as a lunatic. They might have a point.

"You boys want another round?" the bartender asked, pulling Brenner from his thoughts. He looked over and Sticks had walked off towards the restroom. Now was his chance to leave if he wanted. He could walk away and never see Sticks again. But then he thought of the tears, the hug, the words.

"Eh, why not? Bring us another round."

Brenner flipped around on his barstool to survey the crowd. People watching was one of his favorite activities when he traveled. Certain places or institutions in society tend to create sample bias. For example, neither churches nor strip clubs accurately represent a cross-section of a town. A crowd at a bar, however, if large enough, paints a pretty accurate picture of the average member of that town's society.

Brenner noticed a biker leaning against the wall, his black leather jacket stitched with the image of a topless woman holding a snake in one hand and a bottle of whiskey in the other. Two college-aged girls shot pool in the corner, drawing a crowd of all-aged men to stare and drool at the shape of their bodies bending over the table. Brenner noted the extra effort the girls put into arching their lower backs when they shot, fully aware of the effects they were having on their onlookers.

Next were the two young men at the other end of the bar. Brenner recognized the bearded one from the outdoors store. He worked there. The other guy wore sandals, a Grateful

Dead t-shirt, and had his somewhat unkempt hair pulled tightly back in a ponytail. He could catch enough of their conversation to know they were talking about different routes up mountain faces and all the latest climbing equipment.

Brenner didn't know why, but he was jealous of them. For a moment, he wished he could work at an outdoor store—spend all day talking about his favorite tents, showing people how to filter water correctly, maybe even tuning up mountain bikes. Anything but spending ten hours a day trying to save sick animals, knowing that a single mistake, a brief lapse in judgment, could cost not just a life but also his reputation. One misstep, and the clients he worked so hard to help might turn on him—disdain, hatred, maybe even a lawsuit.

As he let the thought settle, he realized he *did* know why he was jealous of them.

Suddenly, at the exact moment in time that it was supposed to happen, the door of the bar swung open and in walked the woman that Brenner was meant to see that night.

"Hope," he whispered, inaudibly.

The girl from the store in Clayton, whose brown eyes had sent Brenner into a trance. The first girl Brenner had looked at with any inkling of desire since the passing of his wife. The girl that Brenner had thought about on more than one occasion—sometimes late at night in his tent—during the first few days of his journey. That girl. Before he could even tear his eyes from her, she turned towards the bar and walked right up to him.

"It's Brenner, right?" Her voice floated from her mouth and danced through the air into his ears, making something warm tingle in his belly.

She remembered my name.

Brenner cleared his throat, suddenly self-conscious that his voice might not sound as smooth as hers. Then he considered how awkward his loud, guttural clearing must have sounded. Then he realized that hesitating any longer would be even worse.

"Brenner it is!" he blurted out.

God, what a fucking idiot…

Hope laughed lightly at his absurdity. She had, no doubt, been around plenty of bumbling idiots in her lifetime who struggled to maintain a conversation with her. Beauty can curse a woman. It rules more men than ugliness, especially in high school and college. Locker room bravado dissolves the moment an adolescent man finds himself face-to-face with an angel.

Not just above-average prettiness. That's easy enough to admire, to approach. What truly unravels a man is once-in-a-lifetime beauty—the kind that doesn't just captivate but wounds, exposing everything he will never have, everything he will never be good enough for.

Perhaps it's a defense mechanism—an instinctive retreat before that beauty can become fleeting, temporary, nothing more than a memory that lingers just long enough to haunt.

Brenner fought to steady himself against the surge of adrenaline that talking to her induced. But being a veterinarian had conditioned him to interact with all kinds of people—clients came in every shape and size. Over the past few years, his social skills had improved considerably, even around attractive women.

"You can sit here, unless you're meeting someone."

"I actually am here to meet someone, but I don't see him yet. You sure you don't mind?"

"Not at all." His heartbeat began to slow. *Of course* she was meeting someone.

"I'll take a whiskey on the rocks. Wells, please," Hope said to the bartender, who in turn walked away to grab a glass. "Didn't you have a dog with you? I thought I saw him with you in Clayton."

"Oh, Sam? She checked in early to the motel. We were having a little marital bickering after days stuck together on the trail."

Hope laughed and rolled her eyes. "I take it 'Sam' is short for Samantha?"

"That's the one. Do you like dogs?"

"Who doesn't?" she asked. Before he could answer she added, "I think it's one of the biggest red flags if someone doesn't like dogs."

"I'd agree."

"Do you have a lot of dogs or just her?"

"I only have her. But I see a lot of dogs every day."

"What do you mean? With your job?"

"Yeah," he laughed, "I'm a vet. While I agree with your statement about red flags, I will admit sometimes I want to teleport to a world with no dogs—just for a few hours to recharge."

"I guess anything can become a grind when it's what you do all day. But being a vet sounds like a dream job to me!"

"It definitely has its moments."

"Sticks!" Hope shouted, greeting the person Brenner suddenly realized she was there to meet, who had now returned from his trip to the lavatory. "Sorry!" she said to Brenner, realizing she had just yelled in his face.

"You're kidding! You two know each other?" Brenner asked, dumbfounded at this irony. Here, in this bar to meet one another were the man he initially thought too odd to share a drink with and the woman he considered to be the most beautiful person he had ever seen, the latter wishing to share a drink with the former. "Am I intruding on a date?"

Sticks and Hope looked at each other and burst out laughing. Sticks finally responded, "She wishes! No, we are just friends, maybe siblings separated from birth, who knows really…"

Brenner felt a surprising sense of relief. Guiltily, he admitted to himself that some hidden part of him—one buried deep where Lily couldn't reach—felt a spark of desire for Hope.

"Alrighty then, my interest is piqued. Tell me how you two know each other."

Hours slipped by as the three of them sat at the bar, talking, laughing, and making up stories about each new patron who walked through the door. They flicked folded straw wrappers through makeshift finger goalposts, debated life and the fleeting nature of true joy, and entertained the possibility that happiness might be waiting just around the next river bend.

Brenner, now inebriated, leaned heavily against the bar, his head propped up by his right fist, hanging onto every word that drifted from Hope's lips.

One topic never surfaced—Lily.

More notably, Brenner didn't think of her. For the first time in months, he passed multiple waking hours untouched by the oppressive weight of hopelessness and loss.

The bar started filling in after a while, leaving not much more than standing room. Brenner and Hope watched the crowd and continued talking. "I wonder why it's so crowded," he said.

"Music!" Hope said back, with a smile.

"Alright, you two behave yourselves. Time to tickle some strings," Sticks said, smiling, as he stood up and pushed his empty chair back to the bar.

Brenner, eyes wide in surprise, watched Sticks walk from them towards the stage, where he greeted the man taking a seat at the drums. He then walked to the back of the stage and began unpacking a guitar that had been carried in by one of the other band members.

"He's an interesting guy," Hope said. "You know, he's been through an awful lot in his life."

"No, I didn't realize that. I just thought he was—"

"Odd?" Hope laughed. "Yeah, me too. But you know, Brenner, sometimes the best people are just a little odd. Take me, for example," she looked at Sticks and then back at Brenner, "You'd never know by looking at me, but I actually have twelve toes."

Brenner gagged on his sip of beer, forcing him to clear his throat before responding, "No you don't." He laughed.

"Okay, fine. I don't. But I promise you I'm odd. I'm just as odd as Sticks."

"Oh, whatever. What's your story anyway, Hope? Surely, you're seeing someone."

Hope smiled, anticipating the compliment, but asked anyway, "Surely? How are you so sure?"

Brenner smiled, turning his body on the barstool to face her more directly. "You are beautiful. When I saw you at the store in Clayton, I forgot how to speak the English language. It almost happened to me again tonight. I'm serious," he added when Hope rolled her eyes, "You just about render me speechless."

"Well, thank you," she responded, blushing. "And to answer your question, I am *not* currently seeing anyone."

"Well, why the hell not? Are all the guys up here crazy?"

Hope chuckled. "I can't account for *all* of the guys up here, but the one I know very well isn't crazy, just a piece of shit."

Knowing where this was likely headed, Brenner asked, "If you don't mind me asking, what happened? We also don't have to talk about it."

"My fiancé cheated on me a few months ago, so I left him."

"I'm so sorry, Hope," Brenner said somberly.

"It's fine. I figure, better now than later, you know? I thought my world ended when I found out, but I'm hoping in time I'll come to think of it as my world beginning. I'm not even close to there yet, but I can feel the sun a little brighter every day. Time heals all wounds and I expect it to heal this one." Her voice shook slightly as she finished speaking.

"I understand that more than you could ever know," Brenner said quietly, staring at the edge of the barstool under and between his legs.

"Oh really? Well, same question to you, Brenner. I take it you are single?"

"Yes ma'am."

"Well, how is that possible, because from where I'm sitting it seems you are also a catch."

Brenner laughed and then sighed. He looked into Brook's eyes. "It's a sad story. Do you have a few minutes?"

"I'm all yours."

Brenner went on to tell Hope about his marriage to Lily, the good and the bad. Hope asked questions here and there but largely just listened to the broken-hearted man sitting across from her lament his tragedy. She cried when he told her Lily drowned.

"Brenner, I am so sorry. I can't imagine going through what you've been through. I feel bad now for complaining about my life. It doesn't even compare."

"On the contrary, I think they seem about the same. We are both mourning the death of a relationship and, in each case, neither one of us had a choice. I couldn't keep Lily from dying and you couldn't stop your fiancé from cheating. For what it's worth, I think cheating is the most horrible thing one person could do to another."

"It is. I guess I see your point, but I would still argue yours is worse."

With first a frown and then a sad smile, Hope pushed her beer away, and leaned towards Brenner. Her hands gently wrapped around his neck, and she hugged him. The gap between them became smaller and smaller, and he began to smell her perfume. His hands, though shaking slightly, found their way to her back and he returned the hug. The two of them remained in tender embrace for several moments. The sights and sounds of the crowded bar seemed to disappear, leaving Brenner and Hope on an emotional island that they were happy to share with each other. Until now, they had been on their own islands, alone.

When they finished hugging and started to separate, Brenner felt Hope's hands holding onto his. He looked into her eyes and found a piece of her heart, one that she was trying to give him. He squeezed her hands back and began to lean in, stopping just short of her mouth to make sure he wasn't misreading the situation. He could feel her breath. She let him linger there, in her space, for another moment before closing her eyes and tilting her head to the side.

When her lips met his, the world stopped spinning. The trouble that had encircled and haunted Brenner like banshees from a dead world for months disappeared in an instant and Brenner's mind felt healthy, clean, and present. For the first time since he started dating Lily, Brenner allowed his soul to touch someone else's, and he remembered there is still good in the world. Outside the boundaries of joy he had established erroneously for himself, a good place may still exist. A place of beginnings, where the old could be buried and forgotten.

After an unknown amount of time—perhaps no time, as time stood perfectly still for each of them for the duration of the kiss—she separated her mouth from his and whispered, "I'm sorry, I don't know what got into me."

"Don't be sorry. I've wanted that since I first laid eyes on you."

Hope blushed and got out of her chair. "I'm going to use the restroom. I'll be right back. Don't go anywhere."

"I wouldn't dream of it." Brenner was left alone, starry-eyed, at the bar. He inhaled deeply, catching the faint trace of her perfume still clinging to his shirt.

Thank God I showered before coming out, he thought.

Then came the shudder—the involuntary chill as thoughts of Lily crept in, uninvited. It felt ironic, didn't it? That she would reach for him—from wherever she was—just before he met someone new.

No. Ironic wasn't the word.

It felt calculated.

Or maybe none of it was real. Maybe it had all been some

extended flashback, a cruel trick of his own mind. Maybe he was finally waking up, getting his head straight again. Maybe he was finally starting to heal.

A few introspective minutes later, Hope reappeared. Her shoulder-length walnut brown hair waved in the air as she looked from him to the band. He found himself wondering if her olive skin was merely tanned from the sun or bestowed by genetics, something the nature of tan lines might discern. Brenner felt slightly guilty for undressing her with his mind. She was, however, the most beautiful woman Brenner could remember ever meeting, as if God made her first, an example to the angels of his ability to craft the perfect creature.

Instead of sitting back down, she held out her hand. "Will you dance with me?"

The two didn't take their eyes off each other for the next hour, something Brenner relished. When the songs were fast, they playfully twirled and shagged. When they were slow, they held each other in close embrace and moved gently in circles, never breaking eye contact, expressing feelings beyond the capacity of words.

The music finally stopped, and Sticks rejoined them, somehow drunker than when he started playing.

"I see they took care of you on stage," Brenner said, gesturing towards the cup in Sticks' hand.

"Music must be played with a certain laxity, otherwise it's too structured and stressful," Sticks replied, laughing. "I take it you two did alright by yourselves, though I'm not sure you behaved."

"Oh, whatever," Hope giggled, playfully pushing Sticks.

"Well, Brenner, it's been a pleasure, my man, but this guy needs to get some rest before joining the workforce once again tomorrow. Good luck with the rest of your journey. Promise me you'll reach out when it's over." Sticks raised his eyebrows, signaling to Brenner he was referring to more than hiking alone.

"I promise, I have your number. Thanks for everything, Sticks. You're a good dude."

Sticks smiled, hugged Hope, whispered something in her ear, and left the bar.

Minutes later, Brenner and Hope made the short walk from the bar to the motel where an eager Bluetick Coonhound was awaiting her best friend's return. When they reached the door, Hope grabbed Brenner's hands, and kissed his cheek. Instead of pulling back, she whispered, "Can we kiss a little more?"

Brenner's stomach lurched, and he closed his eyes firmly and sighed, letting the pause before his response linger and slightly stale. "I really want to. I just—"

"No, it's okay! We just met," Hope responded, looking embarrassed, recognizing the pause could mean a number of things, none of them good.

"No, Hope, it's not that. I just need to take care of something first, on my own." He hated himself, and in a way, he hated Lily—the version of her that currently disallowed him from loving Hope. "Can I call you?" he added quickly, seeing the dejection on Hope's face.

"Yes. Please. I want to continue where we left off," she responded.

"Trust me, I do too."

After getting her number, Brenner pulled Hope into a hug—one that, like their kiss earlier, carried more emotion than words ever could. He started gently, his arms wrapping around her with quiet hesitation, then slowly tightened his hold until he was fully there, holding her like he didn't want to let go. She matched his embrace, her warmth pressing into him, neither of them willing to be the first to pull away. For nearly a minute, they stayed like that—just breathing, just being.

When they finally parted, Hope kept hold of his hands, her fingers lingering against his. Then, with a soft smile, she leaned in and kissed him one last time.

Chapter 14

After a short shuttle ride, more confused than ever, Brenner, with Sam at his side, stepped back onto the Appalachian trail the following day with a slight hangover and the persistent fluttering of Monarch wings in his belly left by a girl that seemed too good even for dream or fantasy. He slept little the night before, considering what fork in the road to embark upon.

Should he follow the path of history and comfortability, chasing the memory of his wife, someone with whom he had shared the better part of his adult life? But who was Lily now? What was Lily now? He repeated the three same words over and over in his mind: *But Lily died.* Yet, she was here. Somehow, he had found her. That had to mean something.

Over the years, Brenner had forgotten the rush of new love—the spark, the possibility, the way it made the world feel alive. The heady romance of early passion had faded, worn thin by the quiet familiarity of marriage. Marriage had been steady, reliable—a comfort, but not a chase. Love hadn't disappeared, but the pursuit had. Slowly, almost imperceptibly, the extraordinary had become commonplace. He had cherished Lily, and in the wake of her loss, he remembered only the good. Yet there had been pain and frustration too. Things had gone so wrong and with Lily gone they could never be put right. The phantom in the woods was likely just his subconscious' way of trying to rewrite the past.

Now, with Hope, as those long-dormant feelings stirred again, as something new pressed against the weight of memory, Brenner let his mind wonder.

And again, Lily was dead.

Hours spent tossing and turning on the thin motel mattress had not yielded a definitive answer or direction other than the decision Brenner would leave no stone unturned. Whatever he would ultimately decide, it wouldn't be tainted by a future doubt that he didn't have enough information at the time of his decision. Thus, even though a large part of him wanted to conclude his journey that very morning, he returned to the trail to find Lily, confront for once and for all whether he was being haunted by the spirit of his dead wife or by just her memory and way too many psychedelic mushrooms. He'd give it a couple more days, if anything, to prove to himself he wasn't crazy. After a seemingly normal night in town, he prayed that he'd realize none of it was real. But one thing was certain—he no longer had any desire to hike the entire state of North Carolina.

Looking at his map, Brenner picked a shelter that was an ambitious, full day of hiking away: Wayah Shelter. Supposedly there would be a lookout tower atop the nearby Wayah Bald and Brenner considered it a deserved reward. Ironically, much of the Appalachian trail, despite following ridge lines, is deprived of sweeping views in the summer due to the heavy burden of leaves upon the hardwood canopy. Climbing a stone tower solves that problem if you have the energy after a day of hiking. The eleven or so miles would be the furthest he'd hiked in a day thus far on the trip, but he felt rejuvenated by real food and drink, despite his restless night.

Unlike her owner, Sam had no inner conflict—only pure, unfiltered joy. She was ecstatic to be back in the woods, free to roam, chasing anything that moved—including the occasional protein-packed grasshopper. Brenner watched as the hound barreled ahead, her body a blur of motion, powered by the kind of carefree joy he could only envy. For a fleeting moment, he wished they could trade places—that he could know such simple happiness. But then he thought better of it. He wouldn't wish his burdens on his best friend. Instead, he let himself take in the moment—watching Sam, enjoying her unbounded delight.

"Hey goofball, let's go this way!" He shouted to her as she ran through the woods away from him, the only part of her visible being the white flag on her ever-wagging tail. When she finally broke off of her route and rejoined him, she "play bowed" and her front paws bounced around on the dirt floor. "What now?" Brenner asked, laughing. Realizing what she was about to do, he quickly tried to add, "No Sam, don't bar–"

Sam barked.

"Samantha!"

Sam barked again.

"Oh okay, I see. Is that how it's going to be?" On the last word, Brenner dove and tackled Sam, partially forgetting his backpack was on. He awkwardly rolled on his side with her in his arms, while she proceeded to lick the morning sweat from his face. "Alright, alright, let's go, girl." He stood up and beckoned her ahead on the trail, the latter satisfied enough with the attention given to go in the direction she had known the whole time to be the correct one.

"Okay Lily, where are you?" Brenner murmured under his breath.

By midday, Brenner was already starting to regret rejoining the trail.

He had set out to heal from losing Lily, and in some way, meeting Hope—and allowing himself to desire her (as if such things were ever truly a choice)—had proven that healing was possible.

So why was he still here? Still hiking, still searching.

For what?

A ghost?

His doubts were growing. It had only been a couple of days since his interaction with his dead wife, but was it possible he imagined the whole thing? Was even Rami real? Was his broken mind playing tricks on him? As he put one foot in front of the other, passing amongst the towering trees and boulders of Southern Appalachia, he considered the terrifying thought that his mind was slipping, that the hallucinogenics and his grief and the physical exertions of the trail had conspired against his sanity. But maybe that was less terrifying than if Lily was really there.

He later stopped for lunch by a small stream and was sucked into a trance by the orchestral sound of gravity pulling water down the mountainside. He stared blankly at the foam line, created by a seam between two currents and thought of nothing at all, letting his mind be still and meditative. Sam rehydrated herself in the creek and napped. Minutes came and went, any sense of hurry gone. Finally, Brenner stood and brushed off his pants.

"Alright, Sam," he started, "I've decided your dad might be crazy. If we don't find your mom by tomorrow morning, we'll go find Hope instead."

With new life in his step—fueled by the relief of having a plan, an endpoint, and the promise of seeing Hope again—Brenner pushed onward, letting thoughts of Lily fade into the background. Instead, he focused on the future. Deep down, he knew it was probably too soon to start a new relationship, but the thought gave him purpose.

I wonder if she is from Franklin. I wonder what her family is like. She likes dogs, the outdoors, camping, live music… and she drinks whisky on the rocks. Who is this girl, really?

As the sun began its slow descent from its peak in the hazy, moisture-laden sky, Brenner and Sam passed a weathered wooden sign: Wayah Shelter 3.4 miles.

With every step, Brenner convinced himself more and more that he and Sam had been alone all along. After all, he didn't believe in ghosts. He was a veterinarian—a man of science. Death was no mystery to him. He saw it daily in his practice, in those final moments when beloved pets slipped from this world with no hope of return. He had seen Lily's body in the morgue, its waterlogged form so battered from retrieval that there had been no open casket viewing.

She couldn't have been here.

For the first time in months, Brenner also began wishing he was at work with Ben. Despite looking forward to a far-off retirement every day he spent in the busy vet clinic, when absent he now felt a touch of lazy uselessness, like his role in life was being pushed aside for personal reasons. He was giving nothing back now. His clients needed him, and he missed the other vets and technicians. As much as he hated to admit it, he even missed—no, craved—the chaos. Yet, here he was, wasting time in the woods, alone, wandering around like a wayward spirit.

Brenner's pace picked up as if he was walking not towards the tower at Wayah Bald, but rather towards the rest of his life. He hiked with haste towards his job, his family, his friends, his home. He considered that he could simply turn around and go back to Franklin, but he decided he'd mark the Nantahala Whitewater Center as his endpoint. It was familiar and he was close enough.

A few hours later, Brenner repeatedly tossed a large stick down the mountainside for Sam to barrel after, sometimes gracefully and sometimes not. As a hound, she was phenomenal at locating but made a poor retriever. Thus, this was the sixth or seventh stick Brenner had found to throw. The dog would generally bring the stick back once or twice, but never three times in a row, often dropping it when her nose found a fresh smell drifting up from the valley below.

"C'mon, girl!" Brenner would call again and again. "We'd be there already if not for you." The day was mostly warm and humid with occasional cumulonimbus clouds, the early attempts at storm cells, passing through the hazy, blue sky. Hence, Brenner was caught off guard when the cool breeze pushed through the trees and circled around him. He frowned and looked in the direction from which it had originated. East. "That's peculiar," he murmured, as the clouds had been moving from west to east all day, which is typical for those latitudes. He didn't see any storm clouds above him, or anywhere on the horizon for that matter. *Lily?*

The air gradually heated back up as the pair made their way closer and closer to Wayah Bald and the lookout tower. The sun had completed its ascent in the summer sky and was now accelerating towards the western ridges of ancient stone.

"There it is, Sam," Brenner said, eyeing the large stone structure erupting from the tree line directly in front of them and slightly uphill. He adjusted his pack and rubbed his shoulders, now starting to grow sore at the intersection of strap and flesh. He winced as he pressed his fingers into the belly of his left shoulder. "I don't know about you, but I think I'm almost ready to get the hell out of here." Sam wagged her tail at the sound of her owner's voice and galloped uphill towards their destination, which she now had also spotted.

With sweat beading up on his brow, Brenner walked with his best friend across the stone patio of the overlook tower, nodding at the only other people at the tower, a couple that was unmistakably newly in love. He immediately noticed the ring on the girl's finger and the dried streaks of tears on her face. A proposal, likely. Though he didn't witness it, he imagined the man on his knee, asking the ultimate question with the backdrop of rolling, never-ending sequential ridges of deep blue, each growing lighter until they were consumed by the distant sky. A good place, he thought. Not that unlike his proposal to Lily.

When the lovers had left the platform, so wrapped up in each other they hardly seemed to notice man or dog, Brenner unloaded his backpack onto the stone floor and climbed up on the ledge to dangle his feet above the forest below. Sam sat near him at a break in the wall so that she too could watch the sun begin to cut the sky open, rendering colors of red and orange that marked the beginning of sunset.

"Without you," Brenner started, causing Sam to look away from the sky and up at him with knowing brown eyes, "I don't know if I could have done this. I mean, not the trip, but the healing. I know you miss her too, sweet girl." He thought about the heartbreaking nature of Sam losing her mom but not knowing why. He wondered if Sam thought she was abandoned by Lily. Like somehow, she hadn't been a good enough dog. He couldn't even explain to her what happened. Dogs shouldn't have to outlive their owners. He climbed down and hugged Samantha, trembling as he stroked her big, soft ears.

"She loved you, Sam. She loved you so much. Maybe even more than she loved me. You were her baby, the only one she got to have," he said as tears filled his eyelids. Sam licked tears from his cheeks. "But you know that, don't you? You know more than I give you credit for. In fact, you're the strong one in this relationship." He continued petting her, putting all of his emotions into the tender strokes on her head and her cheeks, hoping she could feel how much he loved her by how he touched her. He began crying more and more as he sat there, feeling sorry for himself and for his dog. At last, he simply said, "Thank you.

"Alright, Sam. Let's go home, huh? What do you think about that? Let's be done with this place. I don't need to heal anymore. We have each other, don't we?" He scratched her rump and beckoned her forward with him towards the stairs off the platform. "I'll look at the map and find the next crossing."

He had slightly misjudged the time until mountain sunset, when the light disappeared behind the peaks, and thus he and his companion set up camp an hour later by the soft light of headlamp. Once the tent was up and everything was prepared for sleeping, Brenner set a small fire in the stone ring at the edge of the site. After stoking the flames and becoming confident it would stay lit long enough to eat, Brenner poured some kibble into the collapsible dog bowl for Sam and went about boiling water for his freeze-dried ranch chicken, specifically recommended by Sticks.

After his second mouthful—the first was too hot for functioning taste buds—he nodded and planned to thank Sticks should he ever see him again; the chicken was far superior to chili mac. With full bellies, Brenner and Sam sat by the fire for another hour, the latter sleeping soundly on a soft pile of pine straw, a gift from the towering eastern white pines overhead. Brenner stared at the flames, reflecting, occasionally glancing at the steam that evaporated from the shoes he had removed and set against the warm rocks.

The night was silent, devoid of the usual symphony of owls, crickets, coyotes, or breeze. In fact, the only noise that cut through the night air was popping and hissing of the ablaze logs. The teepee-shaped stack of wood Brenner used to get the fire going was still erect and a small hole revealed the bed of embers in the center of the ring. The air funneled through the logs at the hole, creating a swirl of smoke. As cool air moved towards the flames it was directed downward and then lifted by an invisible force up through the center of the logs where it glowed white, then blue, then orange. Finally, it joined the rest of the smoke and was lifted towards the canopy, spreading out and becoming less dense until it all but disappeared.

Brenner was entranced by the fire so much that he didn't immediately notice the air become dramatically cooler. Sam, however, became uncomfortably cold and rose to walk into the tent, claiming a spot inside the sleeping bag. Brenner also didn't notice that he was no longer alone by the fire. Across from him, hidden by the swirls of smoke sat the memory of the woman he fell in love with so many years ago, the person he had loved with every ounce of his being, and the soul that had been lost a few months before, leaving Brenner all but alone in the world he could never imagine without her. Across the fire from the entranced hiker sat Lily.

Brenner's mind suddenly felt heavy, and his consciousness began to slip, one small piece at a time. The edges of his vision became blurry, and he blinked repeatedly, trying to stay awake. As the deeper reaches of his brain started falling asleep, Brenner watched as the smoke above the fire disappeared, wafted away by a hole on its way to another dimension. Left in its wake was the face of his bride. She occupied the only field in Brenner's vision that hadn't been stripped of clarity. He exhaled one last time before sleep overtook him. Lily rose and started walking around the fire towards her sleeping husband.

Chapter 15

"I will lift my eyes up to the hills..."

The Psalm was spelled across the beam above a wooden cross at the end of the chapel. Pretty Place Chapel. The small wooden structure sat on a mountainside, near the border of North and South Carolina, north of Greenville. Behind the cross, the setting sun illuminated the colors of fall, bright reds, yellows, and oranges that were painted on the slopes of the valleys below. A cool autumn breeze rustled a few leaves across the floor and by the man's feet. Was he alone? No.

A young woman knelt by the cross and stared out at the mountains. Her blond hair fluttered in the wind, and she let her head come to rest on her arms, folded on the outer stone wall. The setting sun revealed only the color of her hair, the remainder of her body a mere silhouette. She looked like an angel. The man watched her and smiled, fiddling with something in his pocket.

She turned around and smiled back at him, the sun reflecting a small bit of moisture in her hopeful, adventurous blue eyes. "It's beautiful."

"So are you. I don't think I've ever seen a prettier sight," the man responded, holding his hands up like a frame, with the girl right in the middle.

"Come sit with me," she pleaded. The man strolled to the edge of the chapel and reached his hands down to hold hers. She let her fingers intertwine with his and she squeezed his hands. "I love you so much."

"Stand up," he responded. When she did so, he traded places with her and knelt down where she had previously sat near the cross. Her eyes widened. "Lily, I love you too. Will you marry me?"

***

Brenner smiled as he slept, reliving the memory that had made him the happiest in life. The months that follow a proposal are generally the easiest part of a marriage, despite technically and ironically taking place outside of matrimony. The comfort of knowing your betrothed has promised to be yours for eternity. The weaseling fear of insecurity that the other may decide they want someone else disappears. Normal, commonplace moments are enriched by addresses of "fiancé". "When we are married…" and "One day…" augment the beginning of sentences pertaining to the future joining of lives.

Yet lives are not yet joined and the stress that comes from combining not only your soul, but finances, possessions, time, and feelings with another's still somewhere around a distant, invisible corner. The absence of stress brings happiness, and happiness brings a reduction in stress. Thus, an engagement precedes a period in life that is hallmarked by hopeless optimism and raw love. Such was the case for Lily and Brenner, and while sleeping in a tent deep in the valleys of Appalachia, Brenner dreamed of his engagement.

When Brenner finally woke up, he found himself in the arms of Lily, who tightened her grip comfortingly as his mind processed the moment in which it found itself. He shuddered, but then relaxed and looked into her eyes.

"You," he muttered.

"I was wondering when you'd wake up," Lily whispered. "What were you dreaming about? You looked happy." She smiled and brushed her hair away from her eyes, tucking a particularly golden lock behind her right ear.

"I think you know what I was dreaming about." He looked down at her hands touching the bare skin of his side. "I don't remember falling asleep."

"You fell asleep by the campfire last night. I carried you in here."

"How?" he asked. "And my shirt?"

"Oh, come on, we've been married for three years. I think I've earned getting to take your shirt off." She laughed.

Brenner's stomach turned over and he squirmed, pulling slightly away from her grip, which seemed to be tightening again.

"What?" she asked.

"You said, 'we've been married,' Lily. You…"

"Died? I know. You keep saying that but I'm here, aren't I?"

"I don't understand. I *can't* understand."

"You don't have to, baby. Just trust me. I'm not going anywhere."

Brenner pressed his lips together and his mind wandered briefly to Hope and the advice from Sticks. Lily then caressed the back of his neck, exactly like she always had in the early mornings in their bed back home while he woke up, resetting the attention of his mind and, more importantly, his heart back on her.

"What's bothering you?" she asked, wiping a single tear from her cheek.

"How can we ever go back to what we had before?" Brenner too began crying, seeing bits and pieces of their life together flash before his eyes.

"We just take it one day at a time. That's all we can do."

"I wish I could just wake up. I want it to all just be a dream so badly. I want to wake up next to you, like any other day, before any of this ever happened. Please Lily," he sobbed, "let this just be a dream. Wake me up. Wake me up! Please wake me up, I'm begging you..." Sobs were replaced by soft whimpers as his chest trembled up and down while he struggled to catch a breath and reprieve from the painful gasps.

"Bren, you are awake." Lily cupped Brenner's cheeks and lifted his head up towards hers. "You're awake and I'm here with you. Yeah, maybe it's different, but it's still me. It's still us!"

After a while, Brenner's breathing finally steadied, the gasping and sobbing fading into silence.

He lay still in Lily's arms, his eyes tracing the small birthmark on her neck—just as he had so many times before. She was wearing the pajama pants he had given her last Christmas Eve.

How is she wearing them? She had been buried in her favorite "teacher outfit" as she called it, a flattering bright pink top with black slacks. He knew because her mom had helped him pick the outfit out. So how was she wearing those pants?

The question hovered at the edges of his mind, knocking, waiting to be acknowledged. But he refused to let it in.

Instead, he swallowed hard, exhaled, and finally spoke.

"Okay. I trust you."

Lily slid her hands from his back down his arms and then into his hands. "Okay, let me show you one more!" She giggled gleefully as Brenner's mind started to slip once again.

***

The breeze had the sharp, but welcome, chill of late autumn and small, oblong willow oak leaves swirled in the background, rustling gently while the air hissed through the nearby pine thicket. If not for the pungent smoke that hovered over the nearly-spent bed of coals in the fire ring, the scent of tannins in decaying forest leaf beds, that perfect smell of fall would have been forefront.

"Okay, one more!" Brenner said, smiling at his fiancé, who sat one third of the way around the fire ring from him, cozy in her down jacket, scarf, and oversized beanie. He proceeded to start picking the strings of his wooden guitar—Am, F, C, then G—over and over in a gentle, soulful pattern.

Brenner was never a singer and had known that about himself from an early age. When he asked to sing for his parents, they critiqued his every effort. He had relegated any artistic use of vocal cords to the isolation of his vehicle and his shower. That is, until he met Lily. She heard him sing for the first time when she showed up at his apartment early and found him still in the shower. Apparently, love is both blind and tone deaf because she immediately fell in love with his voice.

Brenner had never met someone who loved him the way Lily did. He could do anything, and Lily would think he was the best at it. So, after much pleading, Brenner sang for Lily, often and passionately.

Around the fire that night, Brenner sang her a new song he had written. In fact, it was the first song he had ever written for and about Lily. She watched through starry, moist eyes as her man described how he felt about his soon-to-be wife through song. She eyed the vein that popped out from beneath the skin on his neck when he got to the chorus.

When he finally stopped and the last chord slowly drifted through the canopy, she walked to him and sat in his lap, forcing Brenner to set the guitar gently against a large stone. "I love you so much, Brenner."

"I love you too… obviously." They both laughed and Lily leaned in for a kiss.

Anyone who has been in a romantic relationship knows that there are three different kinds of kisses. The worst kind is the peck or "pull-away" kiss. Perhaps a better term would be the "finisher". When one lover goes in for the kiss, if the other is not in the mood for kissing—or perhaps not in the mood for more than kissing—they will give the "finisher". Mouth barely open and pulling away as soon as lips touch, the "finisher" signals to the initiator that they will be receiving no more than a single kiss. The second type is the "I love you" kiss. This kiss is true and tender. It communicates love and caring without crossing the line of desire. The third, and final type of kiss, and the one Lily gave Brenner that night, is the passionate, "I want to take your clothes off" kind of kiss.

Brenner, being no fool and well versed in the types of kisses, forgot his guitar even existed and carried Lily, who he continued passionately kissing, into the small green tent.

After a long and beautiful moment, the two lay in embrace under the unzipped sleeping bag staring into each other's eyes, saying things without words for fear that words may somehow alter or cheapen deep, unfiltered emotion.

"I want to be with you forever," Lily said, finally.

"Guess what?" Brenner smiled.

Lily blushed and responded, "What?"

"You get to be." He fondled the diamond ring on her finger, and she squirmed with joy.

***

With a sound like rushing water in his ears, Brenner woke up in the tent, next to Lily, just like in the dream. When his eyes adjusted to the light, he leaned in and immediately kissed Lily. To his surprise, she gave him the "finisher" kiss. His eyes widened and he felt embarrassed, for many reasons.

"What? I can't be that easy!" She slapped his arm and said, "Get up, lazy boy, we've got some hiking to do. Unless you've decided to end your trip…?"

"Okay, okay. Let's go on an adventure." He suddenly sat up and looked around in alarm. "Lily, where's Sam?"

"Oh, she's sitting outside. Don't worry, she'll get used to me."

"She'd better," Brenner responded, raising his eyebrows at Lily.

"She will. Come on, get dressed." She walked out of the tent, now wearing hiking pants and a light jacket.

An hour after breakfast—a meal in which Lily took no part—the three of them, Sam keeping as far from Lily as she could while still staying in sight, crested a ridge on the trail that ended up being a false summit. The real summit was still a few hundred feet in front of and above them. Brenner wiped sweat from his brow and clinched his eyes tightly when he felt the salty stinging. "Damn it, I thought this was going to be the top," he said to Lily, as they both watched Sam effortlessly trot up the next hill. He peculiarly looked at Lily who seemed not to have broken a sweat at all. In fact, she wasn't even breathing heavily. "Do you not get tired anymore?"

"Oh," she started, putting her hands on her knees, "I do. I was just zoning out for a second." She started panting and looked back at Brenner.

Brenner collapsed back onto a large boulder ten feet off the trail and sighed. The breeze drifted in lazy circles through the trees around them, dancing with the leaves and creating a shimmering effect on the mountainside. Lily slowly paced towards Brenner and let her pack slip off her delicate shoulders and fall to the ground. She then leaned next to him on the stone and rested her head on his shoulder. The tingles of butterfly wings pulsed through his belly as he felt her soft hair blow against the side of his face. So fine and blonde. Brenner could barely see it when strands passed over his eyes.

He turned his head and looked at his wife and marveled that he found her somewhere out in the wild. She looked back up at him and smiled softly, putting her hand on the side of his face, caressing his cheek. "Oh, Lily…" he sighed, embracing her in a strong hug, letting his chin rest on her right shoulder. When he did, however, something caught his eye in the distance. There was movement on a low hanging branch of an old, dead hemlock. A bird. Brenner blinked and then squinted his eyes to clear any blurriness. What he saw made his stomach drop and he shuddered. It was the mockingbird.

Lily noticed the shudder and pulled away quickly. When she saw the expression on his face she whirled around and investigated the woods in the same direction he had seen the mockingbird. "What is it? What did you see?" she asked sharply.

"What?" Brenner asked, trying to process how to respond. He lied, "I didn't see anything. I was just thinking about when you died. It broke my heart, Lily. My entire life ceased to exist. I didn't think I'd ever recover."

As the words left him, a new thought settled in—given current circumstances, maybe he hadn't recovered at all.

"Oh. Are you sure that's all?"

"Am I sure what's all?" Brenner furrowed his brow, taken aback by her response. *Why does she care so much about what I've seen?*

"I mean," Lily started, recognizing his concern, "I can't imagine, baby. I never want you to have to feel that ever again." The corners of her lips rose into a subtle, but caring smile. "I'm here now. Your life exists now."

Brenner barely heard the words Lily spoke over the internal dialogue in his mind. He forced a smile and nodded his head, assuming it would be an appropriate response based on the tone she had used to say whatever she had said. "What's our goal for today, Lily? How far do you want to hike?"

"It doesn't matter to me! We don't have to hurry anymore now that we have found each other."

"How about Cold Spring? It looks like it's only a few miles from here. I'm feeling a little tired today," he responded.

Lily studied the map for a moment and then pointed. "It looks like there might be a decent creek at Burningtown Gap. I wonder if there are any fish!"

"You want to fish?" Brenner asked, surprised.

"Well, it's not every day I'm reunited with my husband."

"Alrighty then, we'll fish on the way to Cold Spring shelter, but first we have to climb this damned hill."

Brenner trudged up the mountainside, placing one foot in front of the other, the trail so steep it left him questioning the trailblazer's refusal to include switchbacks. After a few choice curses directed at whoever had designed this route, his thoughts drifted back to the mockingbird.

Logically, he knew all mockingbirds looked more or less the same. But deep in his soul, he felt it was the same one—the same bird from his dreams, from his mushroom-induced vision.

With each step, his heart sank a little further.

If the bird was trying to protect him, that meant he had something to fear. And the only thing he could imagine it warning him about… was Lily.

"Are you okay, sweetie?" she asked from behind him.

"What? I'm fine…" he said, voice trailing off as a sudden wave of exhaustion passed over him. His head trembled gently from side to side as he felt his consciousness slipping. "What's… happ—"

"Brenner!" Lily shouted, rushing forward to catch him as he fell backwards into her arms.

Brenner was on the verge of blacking out, but the moment his back touched Lily's hands, a surge of energy shot through him.

In an instant, reality tore open—and he was pulled into another vivid dream.

***

Dr. Poole sat across a large wooden desk from Lily and Brenner, whose hands were tightly clenched together, hoping that if they kept squeezing harder and harder, the doctor would take it back. Brenner looked at his wife, specifically her eyes, welling with tears. Her lips trembled. She tried so hard to hold it together but now was simply not the time for holding anything together. In one finite sentence, the doctor had just taken away her dreams, her future, and what she clung to as the purpose of her life.

"C'mon Doc, there has to be some way," Brenner pleaded.

"I cannot tell you how sorry I am to be the one to tell you this, but it will be impossible for you to bring a child to term, Mrs. Miles." He frowned and pushed the box of tissues on the table towards the heartbroken young woman. "But that's not to say," he continued, "that you can't have a biological child. Your ovarian reserves are good—IVF and the use of a surrogate is a viable option for someone in your situation."

"Jesus Christ," Brenner said, grabbing his wife by her shoulders. "Look at me, Lily. We will get through this. We can…" He joined her in tears as he searched for the words to say. Instead of finishing his sentence, he held her while she collapsed onto his lap, chest bouncing up and down in sobs.

"I want a baby," Lily whimpered when she caught her breath.

***

With tears in his eyes, Brenner asked, "Why that, Lily? Why did you show me that?"

"I don't know. It just kind of came to me that way. I can't always control what I show you." Lily rested her head against Brenner's chest, and he realized she too was crying.

"Hey, it's okay, we made it past that. You were so tough, Lily. The world threw you its absolute worst and you overcame it, you hear me?" He pressed his lips together and attempted a soft smile. Lily looked up at him and nodded, her eyes finding a calm place somewhere deep in Brenner's. "And we were so close to finding another way…" he added.

The two of them stood there softly embracing one another until Sam came weaving through the trees on their right. She made a wide circle to not approach Lily and came to a sitting position behind where Brenner stood. After a moment of being ignored, Sam gently nudged Brenner's rump and whined.

"Okay, let's get a move on."

Before they started walking, Lily shouted in excitement, "Look!" She then ran over to the base of an old oak stump sitting just off the trail. "Aren't they beautiful?" She knelt and began collecting something from the soil. When Brenner looked down over her shoulder, he saw in her hand a few mushrooms with wavy, convoluted ridges adorning their caps.

"Are those morels?"

"Yes!"

"Since when do you know mushrooms?" Brenner asked.

Ignoring him, Lily put one in her mouth and started chewing. When she swallowed, she groaned, "Ugh, it's so good. Here, try them!"

Brenner reached out and took a couple from her hand, studying the textured topography. After satisfying himself that they did, indeed, appear to be morels, he lifted his hand to throw them into his mouth. At that very moment, there was a rustling that came from a branch high in the towering white pine above them. Brenner, who had paused from eating the mushrooms, squinted as his eyes tried to find the source of the disturbance. By the time his eyes had locked onto the bird, it was merely yards from impact. He gasped as the creature collided with his hand, knocking the mushrooms onto the forest floor. As soon as it had appeared, the bird disappeared, before Brenner was able to identify it.

"Ouch," he muttered as he looked at a small cut on his left hand, near the base of his ring finger, where the bird's beak had struck him.

"Silly birds!" Lily responded, angrily. "Let me get them for you," she continued, squatting below him to pick up the scattered fungi.

"I think I'm good. I don't like mushrooms that much anyway. I had some recently that really didn't agree with me." He frowned. Sam growled.

***

A couple hours later, the trio found themselves looking over the edge of a small wooden bridge into the crystal-clear mountain water below. They had reached the gap and discovered the small stream was well worth fishing. A series of small cascades to their right looked promising, but the real draw on Brenner's attention at this moment was the sound of a waterfall to their left, somewhere downstream.

"I got another one!" Lily called from around a small bend only five minutes after they started fishing.

"Damn, Lily. You're crushing it." Brenner himself hadn't even seen a fish. "I'm going to wander downstream and see if I can't find the waterfall."

"I'll be right behind you."

The bank was too covered in rhododendron to traverse, so Brenner was forced to trudge slowly through the creek along the uneven bed of stones, small and large. He envied the dog who somehow effortlessly wove her way through the foliage. When at last Brenner found the source of the sound, he was disappointed. There was indeed a waterfall, only it was significantly taller than what he would have thought possible for this creek. As much as he'd like to try his luck in the pool at its base, there was no way down. He sighed and began to turn around to head back towards Lily.

"Shit!" he shouted, when he turned around to find her immediately behind him, close enough he could reach out and grab her. "When the hell did you get here? I didn't even hear you!" She opened her mouth to speak but he interrupted her. "It doesn't matter anyway, it's impassible," he said, pointing with his rod at the steep drop where water disappeared from their plane to one far below.

"Are you sure?" she asked him, eyeing the precipice over his shoulder. "I want to look."

"Be careful," he responded. "It's pretty damned steep."

"I'll be alright, thanks," was her curt response.

Brenner couldn't help himself and followed her to the edge, grasping her hand to steady her as he approached her side.

"I think we could make it, Bren. And we know there are fish down in that pool."

"No, Lily. We are absolutely *not* going to climb down. Come on, let's go back."

Sam whimpered and stole Brenner's attention. He watched as she stood up and walked to a spot near him on the bank. She turned her head to look back towards the trail and whimpered again.

"I know girl, we're coming." He looked back towards the fall and said, "Lily, let's go," but not before she began descending the slippery rocks at the head of the falls. "Goddamnit, Lily!" He rushed towards her and grabbed her wrist. A fuzzy feeling started at the base of his skull as he felt his mind slip. "Not now!" he yelled aloud, perhaps to Lily and perhaps to himself. Adrenaline pumped through his veins, and he suppressed whatever vision from their past might be coming.

Lily took another step down the face of the waterfall, causing Brenner to panic. *She's really doing it*, he thought frantically to himself. "Lily, I'm begging you, stop it!" Just then she lost her balance and started sliding away from Brenner, only held up by his hand that desperately clung to her arm. The weight was too much for Brenner's grip alone and he felt himself sliding with her in an effort not to let her fall. Within seconds, they both started tumbling over the rocky face.

For whatever reason, people describe the sensation of their life flashing before their eyes during a near-death experience. Brenner experienced no such thing, but instead worried only for his dog, who might soon be alone in the middle of the mountains.

Somehow, Lily was finally able to latch onto a rock and stop herself. Brenner released her arm and slowed himself enough to find a rock to plant his foot against. He stared down thirty feet to the base of the waterfall, knowing the water was shallow and only barely covered the jagged stones underneath its surface. After catching his breath, Brenner saw that Lily had made it to safety beyond the top of the falls. Partially relieved, he started the methodical climb back towards her. Though he had only slid eight or nine feet, one more slip and he might find himself hurling towards the fate that lay below him.

Suddenly he heard a series of barks and guttural growls from the top of the waterfall. Sam proceeded to produce noises Brenner never imagined she was capable of making. "Sam!" he yelled as he forced himself finally over the stone rim at the top. Lily rested against a tree across from the dog, visibly exhausted and distraught. Sam, with hackles raised, continued growling at her.

"Honestly, Lily, I don't fucking blame her! What the hell was that?"

"I'm sorry," she whispered. Her hair was drenched and hung over her downturned face.

"I don't even know what to say." Brenner fumed in the direction of his wife. A few moments of silence later, he finally said, "Let's go find somewhere to set up camp. I need to dry off." The young man and his dog waded back upstream towards the safety of the wooden bridge and dry ground while Lily stared at them. Eyeing them up and down, she looked disappointed, even irate. Finally, she shrugged, smiled and rose from the ground, hair already looking drier.

The walk to find a spot suitable for camping was silent, apart from the sound of boot and paw on dirt. The sun had reached its peak several hours previous and was now accelerating towards the western horizon, painting dark outlines of trees along the trail that meandered ahead, seemingly forever. Brenner decided that he would never have the desire to hike to its conclusion in Maine. This section was long enough, and with every step, it seemed to stretch farther, as if time itself had lost its grip. He no longer felt like he was moving forward from one day to the next but instead trapped in a single, unending moment—a loop outside the normal flow of time, neither past nor future, just an infinite, circular now. And so, he kept moving forward, his hound at his side, covering more ground than he expected. Each step brought him closer to the end—something he had begun to crave.

The early evening was surprisingly cool and finally Brenner decided it was time for a fire. He found a decent clearing in the woods with a bed of pine needles and began pitching the tent. "Would you mind setting a fire?"

"I don't know how," Lily responded, embarrassed.

"Fine, I'll do it. Can you at least help get the tent up?"

"Of course."

After Sam went to sleep in the tent, Lily and Brenner sat together by the fire. Brenner's eyes were glazed over, staring in the direction of the flames gently licking the pine logs. He could feel Lily's eyes burning a hole in him. She hadn't said anything while he ate, and she asked for no food. She just stared.

"I said I'm sorry. I didn't mean to… to fall."

"I don't think you meant to fall. I'm just wondering if you meant to—"

"Meant to what?" She shot him a questioning glance.

"I don't know. It's just… something doesn't feel right, Lily. You have to feel it too, don't you?"

He frowned. "It's not supposed to be this way. We were in love—the kind of love that makes your heart ache, that fills every waking moment with hopeless, desperate longing for the other person. Was it perfect at the end? No. But even then, it was the kind of love that made it seem like if it ever ended—if, for any reason, we were torn apart—our lives would simply cease to exist. Our souls would have to start over, stripped of even the most basic understanding of love, knowing we'd likely never find it again."

His voice broke, and tears filled his eyes. "We would hope," he choked out, "that maybe God made more than one soulmate for each person in case they lost the first. We wouldn't know it, of course—how could we? But we would hope."

He paused, breath hitching, before finally looking up at Lily. "And you know what? You brought me there—to that point. When you foolishly sacrificed your life that night, my greatest fear became my reality. I've been so angry, and I've been so unbelievably sad. And I have been hoping. I came out here to heal, to believe that maybe I could find a part of me that still wanted to trust in love again, even after what it did to me."

He exhaled shakily.

"And in doing so, I seem to have found you."

His eyes searched hers, filled with equal parts grief and desperation. "I don't know what you are, but I do know one thing: we were in love in life, Lily. This isn't life. I don't know what this is, but it's not the same. I want it to be. I long for it to be. I even pray for it to be. But it's just not."

His voice cracked as he met her gaze. "How can you not see that?"

Lily, with wet eyes, stood and walked to Brenner's chair and collapsed into his arms, pressing her head against his chest and stroking his back with her soft fingers. "I know, Bren. Just breathe, it's going to be okay. I don't know how, but I promise it will." They sat together long enough that their breaths slowed and synchronized. Brenner, grasping at something—anything—tangible, squeezed Lily tightly.

After caressing his head and running her fingers through his greasy hair, she reached down and grasped the edges of her light jacket and the shirt beneath, pulling them gently up her torso, revealing first her belly, bronze and soft in the warm light of the fire, and then her bra, holding the weight of her breasts. She then wriggled her arms out and dropped the clothes to the ground under the chair.

"What are you doing?" Brenner asked, looking down at her bare flesh.

She looked deeply into his eyes with a passionate longing as she unclipped her bra from behind her back and let it slide with the weight of gravity down from her chest to her waist. "Do you want me to stop?" she asked softly into his left ear, leaning in closely. She smelled like Brenner's favorite perfume, one that he had given her on their first anniversary date.

"I just don't…" he started, feeling his heart racing in his chest, thumping on his rib cage and reverberating through not only his, but now Lily's bare chest that was pressed against him. "No, don't stop," he exhaled. His mind raced as he wrapped his arms around her waist. She began kissing him, with short, playful pecks, grabbing his bottom lip between hers, repeatedly.

"Let's go get in the tent." Lily stood and Brenner watched her slowly slide her pants off as she walked towards the tent. She was completely naked when she turned around and said, "Come get me, Bren." She unzipped the tent only enough to crawl on her hand and knees through the opening. With apprehension vanishing, Brenner followed her.

When he was fully through the door, Lily grabbed him and pushed him backwards onto his back, jumping on top of him to continue kissing. After a few minutes, she unfastened his belt and started sliding his pants off, letting her knuckles drag against him. Chills ran through his body as he felt her touch. Once he was also completely naked, Lily climbed onto him and prepared to take him in. Her eyes pierced all barriers and touched a place deep within Brenner that he had forgotten existed. Then they became one.

As soon as Brenner felt Lily around him his ears began ringing with a noise that seemed to originate from inside of him, one that made it hurt to be alive. He tried to suppress it, but it only grew louder and sharper until he felt like his head would burst. "Ahhhh! Make it stop!" he shouted, tightly gripping his ears with both hands. "Lily!"

She pinned him down and her eyes burned with a color Brenner had never seen, a color that nobody had ever seen. Almost green, but bright and dim at the same time, her eyes shimmered and engulfed Brenner's entire field of vision. He felt any hope and happiness be forcibly ripped from him, leaving a hole in the center of his soul. His midsection felt as though it had been pulled from him through the ground and was extending towards bedrock. He wished suddenly that he would die.

At that moment, the ringing stopped, and Lily started speaking with multiple voices, encompassing three octaves. Brenner could not only hear her voice but feel it. "You disloyal shell of dust and shit, your soul withers away with or without your knowledge or permission. You have given a piece of your heart to another, and I will see to it that you are trapped in a real, living hell with me, your dead wife!" In her eyes, Brenner saw another woman. "Hope. Is that her name? I promise you that slut will meet me before the end!"

Lily shrieked in rage and looked away from Brenner, allowing him a moment to free himself from her.

"You BITCH!" she howled at Samantha, who had grown tired of tolerance and bit deeply into Lily's hip.

"Sam!" Brenner shouted, as he heard his dog let out a long, haunting yelp of pain.

All at once he knew it wasn't Lily, it had never been Lily. Even if Lily could drag him down a cliff to his death, she could never hurt Sam.

The creature struck Sam once more before Brenner was able to push it away and grab the hound and the half-empty backpack.

Once clear from the tent, he reached into the fire and grabbed a burning log. "Don't you touch my fucking dog!" He heaved the log towards the tent, unfortunately missing, and ran, sprinting alongside Sam in no particular direction other than simply away. Brenner tried to ignore the blood-curdling screams echoing into the night sky. Several sleeping birds awoke and flushed from surrounding trees, flying with panic away from a sound not produced by the living.

Chapter 16

Dogs are extraordinary creatures, often surpassing their human counterparts in virtue and goodness. Unlike people, who are consumed by the chaos of ambition, responsibility, and uncertainty, dogs live just one step removed from the wild, untethered by the burdens of money, progress, or regret. Instead, they concern themselves with simpler, truer things: food, water, shelter, family, and companionship.

The latter two define the essence of the human-canine bond, a relationship as ancient as civilization itself. Humans and dogs became domesticated alongside each other, shaping one another in ways both profound and instinctive. And our species are still intertwined. Puppies grow up viewing their owners as parents, protectors, and providers, looking to them for everything—from the security of a full dinner bowl to the quiet confidence needed to navigate the world.

In return, dogs give their people something far rarer—unwavering loyalty, unfiltered love, and a steadfast presence in an ever-changing world. Anyone who owns a dog knows it is more than just a parent-offspring bond. Dogs look to us as their best friends. They would rather be by our side than anywhere in the world. Their eyes open in the morning and look first to us. We are also the last thing they see at night. In a way, we are their entire world. Some people understand that. The others are not deserving of dogs.

Brenner loved Sam with such fervor that he looked at her and saw a large piece of himself, a piece that seemed like it had always been there and always would be. She wasn't merely a dog, or even the child substitute that she had been for Lily, but an extension of himself, his heart, and his soul. Her eyes reflected the good in the world that is often fleeting. They made him feel loved, needed, and cherished when life threw him aside.

Shaking from sprinting an unknown distance in an unknown direction away from the horror of that night—the horror of the demon masquerading as Lily—Brenner rested his hands on his knees and searched his and Sam's surroundings. When he finally determined that Lily was nowhere to be seen he quickly threw on some clothes and turned his attention to his dog. When he did so, he noticed Sam had collapsed and was breathing heavily in lateral recumbency ten feet from him.

"Sam!" he shouted, running to her side. He felt her heartbeat and then her left femoral pulse, noticing it to be bounding and somewhat thready. He leaned his ear close to her chest to hear her heart and her lung sounds. With his left ear pressed to her his eyes caught something reflecting light from the full moon off the forest floor. Sam was bleeding. She was bleeding a lot.

"No, no, no!" Brenner started, looking for the source of the blood. "Please God, don't take her too..." His eyes started pouring tears and he wiped them as he continued looking for the source of blood that now wet the forest floor extending back from where they had run. There were no wounds on her chest. Brenner's fingers frantically slid down to her abdomen, expecting to find a hole every passing inch. Nothing. He squinted to see better in the dark and through weeping eyes, now also panting in panic. He gently flipped her over onto her left side and immediately saw that the fur on her right lower abdomen and inner right leg were also reflecting the moon. The horrific realization hit him before he even moved his fingers to check. Sam had a lacerated right femoral artery and was bleeding to death.

His hand was quickly soaked in warm blood when he found the defect. Lily, or whatever the hell was in the woods with him, had created a gash on the inner surface of Sam's right thigh. A square inch of tissue seemed to be missing, and her artery pumped relentlessly through the opening. The wound and its placement were intentional, meant to kill the hound dog.

"Samantha, it's okay. It's going to be okay! Please, God, it's going to be okay! I can't lose you." Sam continued panting, but her eyes seemed to glaze over and stare forward. Other than her chest rhythmically filling and emptying, the dog seemed unresponsive and still. Brenner knew very well that a femoral artery tear should have killed his dog already and she was on her way across the short bridge that connects this life to the next. Either from panic or exhaustion, Brenner felt his vision begin to blur at the periphery and his ears began to ring. *No, not now.* He fought it, but soon the world started spinning. He found himself staring up at the sky, hoping to see something that would help him. The moon twirled in circles above him, and he fell backwards, coming to rest on the ground next to his dog.

She's just a patient. Treat it like a patient. You can do this. Brenner didn't know if it was his voice or words from Heaven but when he felt them, he regained enough strength to sit upright once again. Slowly the world stopped spinning and Brenner regained his balance. The tears stopped and he focused on his heartbeat, willing it to slow, if only by a fraction.

He quickly pressed the fingers of his right hand into the defect on Sam's thigh, trying to hold pressure on the bleed while he considered his options. *C'mon, think, think, think…* He knew he had Quik Clot, a kaolin-impregnated cloth that when pressed to a wound and activated would activate clotting cascades and stop bleeding, but he worried it would not cauterize a femoral artery, the biggest peripheral artery in the body.

Brenner had only ever seen one true femoral artery laceration and by the time the dog had made it to the clinic it was too late. The dog had run through barbed wire coming back from a duck blind deep in the swamp. The owner had collapsed through the door, bloody dog sliding out of the old man's arms onto the floor in front of reception. Brenner and his technicians worked for an hour to isolate and ligate the vessel while the dog breathed oxygen from a mask. By the time the artery was tied, the Labrador had begun agonal breathing, eyes glazed over and fixed forward towards the boundary between this life and the next. Brenner listened as the dog's heart slowed little by little until the beats stopped. Everyone in the treatment room sat with silent tears until at last Brenner kicked a bowl across the room and cursed God.

Sam's injury was acute, and Brenner knew there was no way the artery was completely severed, as she would not have retained enough blood to run through the woods, meaning the artery would still be in the same anatomic location as it is in health, not retracted back towards the inguinal ring and abdomen. However, this was not a veterinary clinic. This was the middle of the woods. No oxygen. No suture. No cautery. No technicians. No hemostats—*Wait, there are hemostats!*

Upon this realization Brenner frantically crawled a few feet away to his backpack and found the pocket that held his fishing accessories. His fingers bounced erratically from one object to the next as he searched for the hemostats. He finally felt the rubber gripping and pulled them from his back. "Hang in there, girl!" he shouted as he made his way back to Samantha. She lay still, but still breathed shallow, weak breaths. They weren't sterile and certainly weren't surgical hemostats, having been made specifically for fly fishing, but they were his only shot at grabbing the vessel. He also grabbed his headlamp and a 4x tippet ring, holding the small monofilament typically tied onto the end of fly line.

Breathe, Bren. Once back to the side of his best friend, Brenner turned on his light and began evaluating the wound, occasionally pausing to wipe away fresh blood and apply pressure. It was a bloody mess, and the vet struggled to see anything clearly, least of all the bleeding artery. He needed something to soak up enough blood to see where fresh blood was coming from, rather than digging around in a red pool. He quickly pulled his shirt off and pressed it into the wound, watching as it pulled Sam's blood away from his hand and up almost to the edges of the fabric. He would have to be fast when he removed the shirt, as the blood would immediately fill the hole again.

He took a deep breath and looked up to God, asking for whatever help he would bestow. *Okay… One, two, three!* The shirt was pulled away and the geyser was immediately visible, coming from a small triangular depression between several muscle bellies. Immediately Brenner pushed the hemostats into the wound and attempted to grab the artery. The blood continued spurting even when the jaws of the instruments were closed, meaning he'd missed. The wound was becoming saturated again. Brenner opened the jaws and tried again, missing once more. He would give it one last try before having to remove more clothing to try to clear the field again. He somewhat randomly grabbed a healthy bite of tissue with the hemostats and began taking his socks off. His arms and hands shook violently as the second sock came sliding off the end of his blistered foot.

He focused his attention back on the wound, this time noticing that the pool of blood was small, looking the same as it did before the last grab of tissue. *Could it be?* Brenner soaked up the blood with his socks and started crying in relief when he saw the hemostats clamped securely around the artery. No more bleeding. He prayed a quick "thank you" and then unwound some of the tippet. Within moments, he had hand-tied several Miller's knots around the artery on the side closest to the body and one below the hemostats. "The moment of truth," he whispered, as he carefully released the instrument and pulled it out of the wound. Still no bleeding.

Brenner wanted to collapse from exhaustion but pressed forward anyway. He found the Quik Clot and opened the package. Even though the artery wasn't pumping blood anymore, he knew Sam's blood pressure was weak from the hemorrhage and wanted to do everything he could to facilitate clotting in case his ligatures failed. "I'm sorry, girl," he said, before pressing the fabric into the wound. For the first time since she collapsed, Sam lifted her head and let out a haunting moan as she felt the burn of chemical cauterization. Brenner was happy to see her reaction, even though he knew it was due to excruciating pain. *She's not dead yet.*

Now all that remained was attempting to close the wound. Brenner found the largest fly in his box and used the hemostats to pull away all the feathers and hair, leaving him with a bare hook. He then crushed the barb. He unspooled a much longer measure of tippet and threaded it onto the hook. One bite at a time, he passed the hook and line through the margins of skin on either side of the wound and brought the edges together, placing makeshift sutures until finally the dog's leg was closed. When the last knot was tied, he felt the adrenaline leave his body and he collapsed face first onto his dog. His head rising and falling with each of her barely living breaths and arms wrapped around her torso, Brenner fell into a deep sleep.

In the sleeping world, Brenner dreamt of happiness, somewhere around the corner, a place free of pain and suffering. He dreamt of laying on a beach with the salty air blowing through his hair and wafting evil spirits away before they could ensnare him. In his right hand was a half full Corona Light with a lime floating atop the clear, gold lager. His hand held the bottle with such laziness and lack of care it barely remained lifted above the silty, white sand below. He raised his head from the back of the chair and looked around him. Behind him, dunes rolled endlessly with soft grasses swirling to and fro. In front was the deep blue ocean, extending out far beyond the horizon. His heart jumped when he looked to the left. Sam lay sleeping peacefully and healthily in the sand beside him, feet gently twitching, caught up in some wonderful dream herself. Lastly Brenner looked to the right. Feet gently buried in the sand, sunglasses resting over closed eyes, hair fluttering with each gentle gust, sat Hope.

Brenner heard the seagulls chirping back and forth to each other. The longer he listened, the more he began to realize they didn't sound like seagulls at all. They sounded like mockingbirds. Sure enough, circling directly over him were twenty or so mockingbirds forming a funnel as they drifted down in tighter circles towards him. The leading bird finally came out of the spiral and flew straight at Brenner's face.

Brenner jolted awake in the woods and jumped backwards when he saw a mockingbird on top of his dog, his pillow just moments before. It started jumping up and down on Sam's chest. "Sam!" Brenner shouted when he noticed his dog was not breathing. He felt her chest for a heartbeat and there was none. Sam had gone into cardiac arrest. But she was still warm. The bird flew away to a low limb of a nearby tree.

"Please, Sam! Wake up!" Brenner began compressions over Sam's heart, letting her rest on her side while he furiously pushed against her rib cage with outstretched arms and interlocked fingers. His tears collected on the bridge of his nose and dripped collectively with each downward compression onto his hands. He started speaking aloud to God, "If you made her life, I know you can save it! If you love me at all, please save my dog. I'm begging you!" His voice trembled and he continued pleading until he couldn't think of anything else to say. Several minutes went by and Brenner began to remember statistics on survival of patients in arrest correlated with chronicity: time. He started doubting. He first doubted that Sam would come back. Then he doubted if he would ever come back, if it would be possible for him to survive, physically or spiritually. Lastly, he doubted God. No loving God would do this to him.

Brenner gave up and fell to his knees, hands grasping bits of Sam's fur. "Please just let me die," he cried at the sky. At that moment, the dog jolted violently. She then shook her head and opened her eyes. Unable to lift her head, Sam looked up at her best friend through the corners of her eyes. Brenner once again saw the good parts of life, hidden somewhere past that almond glow of hope and love. He hugged her neck and started kissing the side of her face, eventually leaving his gasping, half open mouth on the fur of her neck.

After an hour of Brenner watching Sam breathe, hoping she wouldn't arrest again, the latter rose to her elbows and lifted her head off the ground. *She might make it.* He knew that even if she lived, she wouldn't be able to hike for several days, until her body replenished enough red blood cells. They would have to wait here, well away from the trail. Brenner wasn't sure he would be able to find the trail and knew he and Sam were lost in the woods, but that was a problem that could be addressed later. Now, he needed to prepare for them to stay here for a few days.

There was a natural cut on the side of the hill beside them, one that Brenner could use to build a very basic lean to. He started by finding fallen pine logs in the forest around him. He wedged them into the ground and let them rest on the hillside just above the depression. Within an hour he had laid an adequate amount of brush over the roof of the shelter, and it was completed. It was nothing fancy, but it would work. He carefully dragged Samantha through the door of the shelter and returned to get his backpack. A large gurgling from his stomach reminded Brenner of his hunger. When he crawled into the shelter, he opened the bag of jerky and pulled a piece out. He held it in front of his dog. The hound's nose wiggled, and she sniffed the air a few times but finally looked at the jerky with disinterest. "Okay, girl. I won't eat until you do." He placed the jerky back into the bag. He had hoped feeding her something salty would encourage her to drink. Instead, he spent the next thirty minutes trying to coax her into drinking by continuously placing the bowl next to her mouth.

Sam fell asleep and began snoring, a welcome sound. Brenner winced when he looked at her back right leg, but not only because it was still covered in blood; he knew the leg would have to come off if, and when, they made it home. It wouldn't survive without blood supply from the femoral artery. In fact, the tissue inside was already dying, and Brenner knew it was only a matter of time until there was tissue necrosis and infection. Of course, there was nothing he could do now besides wait for the leg to become a problem. Sam couldn't walk and he couldn't carry her all the way back. If they fell, or even just tried before she was ready, she could go into arrest again. She needed time. So, Brenner just sat and watched her, hoping their friendship wasn't near its end.

A light shower passed through the mountains in the mid-afternoon and gently wet the top of the shelter, but not the inside. The sound of tiny water droplets crashing on millions of leaves entranced Brenner, and he tried to pick out the sound of one drop on one leaf. He massaged his feet, sore from the barefoot escape through the woods, while his mind wandered to Sam as a puppy. He pictured the way she used to climb on top of her crate only to jump off, time after time, small tail wagging so vigorously it could barely be seen. At night when he asked if she was "hungry", Sam would throw her head back, ears hanging down the sides of her neck, and let out a small, but mighty "arroooo!" His favorite memory of Sam as a puppy was her first interaction with a rabbit. As a hound dog, Brenner worried about Sam immediately killing the first rabbit she ever saw. He walked closely behind her in their yard to ensure she couldn't jump on one without him seeing. Lily would have hated to see her dog kill a "cute bunny".

One day Brenner and Lily were arguing about something, likely—since Brenner could never remember—something meaningless, in the doorway of the garage. Before they could stop her, Sam bolted past them and shot like an arrow to the back right corner of the yard, a place they all, Sam included, had seen rabbits the preceding evening. Lily and Sam sprinted after her, but on account of each only having two legs and not four, could do nothing but watch when Sam reached the unsuspecting rabbit.

The bunny hopped back and forth, trying to figure out which route to take away from the corner. To Brenner and Lily's surprise, when the puppy reached the rabbit, instead of pouncing on it, Sam started play-bowing. Her tail wagged and she matched the rabbit's bounces with bounces of her own. She barked a couple times and looked back at her owners who had now caught up. She ran in circles and urged the bunny to join her. Finally, the rabbit had had enough and instead of bouncing past the puppy jumped over the fence behind it and sprinted away. "Some rabbit dog you're going to make," Brenner said, laughing.

***

Sam yawned and started licking her lips, exerting much effort to painstakingly pull herself up to her elbows once more. She looked at Brenner, who came back from his memories and smiled at his dog. "Hey girl, you look a little brighter, don't you?" It was more of a statement than a question. She gently licked her lips and sighed. Brenner poured some water from one of his bottles into her collapsible bowl. She looked at the water and groaned. "You have to drink some, Sam. It will make you feel better." He paused for a moment and felt a few tears of exhaustion begin to wet his eyes. "Please, Sam."

Sam cocked her head to the side and seemed to recognize how important this small act was to her best friend. Even though she felt tired and didn't want to put effort into drinking, she did it for Brenner. He grinned as he watched her lap up gulp after gulp and imagined her veins and arteries filling up. "That's my girl." Brenner found the small bottle of cephalexin he had brought in case of minor scratches or puncture wounds. Aware that it wasn't the ideal antibiotic for such a serious injury with a risk of sepsis, he removed three capsules and forced them into Sam's mouth, holding her muzzle until she swallowed.

The sun began to set and cast ever-longer shadows that extended out from the base of the trees like souls, trying to escape from the bark. As it burrowed into the horizon, bits of light were asymmetrically caught up in the clouds that draped the mountainside and cast in radiant beams of deep oranges and purples that ran across the sky towards Brenner's and Sam's humble, quiet campsite. The evening felt cooler than the night before—or perhaps Brenner didn't notice the bite in the air the preceding night due to the happenings—so the crackling of wood and embers danced in the night air.

Brenner looked west at the sunset and then back to what he now realized was northeast, the direction from which they had fled the night before. He peered over the tree line at the ridges in that direction and tried to remember how far he and Sam had run. For some reason he had no guess as to how much time passed the night before, like the creature had consumed it from the very fabric of the universe and sequestered it in a singularity centered on itself. It had eaten time. Brenner shuddered. *Well, I know which general direction. I just don't know how far.*

"Hopefully you'll be ready in the morning," he said to the hound, "because I don't know about you, but I'm ready to get out of here. It's time to go home." His heart sank when he considered that the demon wasn't necessarily trapped in the mountains. What if it could follow them home? It would undoubtedly know where it was, it had all of Lily's memories. Even if it didn't follow them, what kind of life would it be if Brenner had to stay away from the mountains?

As if to confirm that she too was ready to abandon this hell, Sam even ate a few bites of her kibble before falling asleep for the night. Brenner laid back against the soft floor of the pine thicket and laid his unzipped sleeping bag across himself like a giant quilt. Sleep came easy and Brenner let his mind slip away, while listening to the soft chirping of crickets mixed with the occasional loud cicada strum. The last thing his eyes saw were the sporadic illuminations of fireflies in the dark air. *This place seems safe.*

***

His eyes opened in a dream of his wedding day. He stood at the front of a long aisle, hands gently clasped in front of him.

He smiled and watched Lily glide towards him, passing pews of admiration. Behind him stood his father and his two best friends, Rami and Sticks. *Wait, what?*

Lily released her father's hand and took her place in front of him, eyes glistening like new stars outshining their peers in the night sky. "Hey, handsome," she whispered as she took his hands on cue from the minister.

"Hey, love. We're doing it."

Lily blushed and squirmed in place.

The minister continued with the words of welcome and introduction. Brenner periodically squeezed his bride-to-be's hands and felt her fingers tighten in response. "1st Corinthians 13: 4-8 tells us that love is patient and kind..."

As Brenner listened to the words of scripture, he started having a nagging feeling in his mind that he knew that voice from somewhere. It was welcoming, it was friendly, it was even... saving? He tried to look at the minister, but his face was covered by a hood. He looked back at his groomsmen to see if they felt the same strange feeling that had come over him. His father made eye contact first and gave Brenner an encouraging thumbs up as if to say, "You've got this, son!" Sticks very slowly mouthed, "Righteous dude..." Brenner's eyes widened when he looked towards Rami. Rami was not there; he had disappeared.

Disconcerted, but realizing he should face Lily, he turned back and locked gaze with her. She furrowed her brow, wondering what on Earth he was doing. Brenner shrugged and tried to ignore the desperation he felt in regard to remembering whose voice the minister was speaking with. No matter how hard he tried to distract himself with thoughts of the reception, the wedding night, the honeymoon, Brenner could not escape the nagging.

When his ears began to ring, Brenner finally turned to the minister and shouted, "Who are you?!"

The crowd began murmuring in horror and Lily's mouth gaped open as she looked at her husband in disbelief and then apologized to the minister. The minister responded to her gesture before she could speak. "Oh, don't worry child, it's quite alright." As he spoke, he allowed his hood to slide back enough that Brenner could see his nose, or rather, his beak. Brenner gasped as he saw the beady, black eyes of a mockingbird looking back at him. "Anyway, that's a perfect segue. It is now time for vows. I've been told that you've each prepared your own?"

"That's correct," Lily responded eagerly. "I will go first." She looked and Brenner saw a small tear run down her left cheek. She smiled. "Brenner Miles. You are so many things to so many people. To your mother, you are a fierce defender against the ever-present heckling from your father." There were several chuckles in the crowd. Brenner's mom playfully punched his dad in the arm.

"To your father, you are the object of his pride. He watches you with the satisfaction and joy that comes with knowing he passed to you his very best traits. You are hardworking, you are morally resolute, you are competitive." Several more hushed laughs.

"Bren, to your friends, you are the energy that binds and pushes relationships forward. If you allowed it, I'm sure half of your friendships would die without the love and passion you bring. You hopelessly pursue relationships with no expectation of repaid pursuit, meaning you want friendships as much for the friend as for yourself. To your dog, Molly, you were her world. She looked at you with her heart, rather than her eyes. It is a look that you freely gave back to her, all the way until the end." Several in attendance, including Brenner, smiled sadly and dabbed their eyes, as Molly had passed away several months prior to the wedding.

Lily continued, "To your clients and coworkers, you are a savior. You take the broken and sick and pour all of yourself into not only healing but loving them. You are the light in a dark room. You bring hope."

"To me, Brenner Miles..." Several people in the room could now be heard sniffling. "To me, you are all of these things." She looked up from her tear-stained notecard and into Brenner's eyes. "I love you and want to be all these things for you. Because I'm not sure…" Lily's voice choked and she quickly ran her arm over her eyelashes, "that anyone has been all these things for you. I need you to fill my cup when it has been drained, and in return, I want to fill yours. I promise to you I will love you, and only you, for the rest of my life."

The words cut Brenner's sleeping heart to the core. While he stood there in front of the crowd of friends and family, he felt the burn of a knife twisting in his gut. He didn't understand why he felt this way. Lily was the love of his life. Why did he now want to run away? He looked at her and saw the corners of her mouth falling, millimeter by millimeter, as the disappointment from his pause grew with each second. He looked around for help but suddenly everyone had disappeared, and he was now standing in a lone beam of light with Lily and the minister. The minister opened his beak and whispered, "Run, Brenner. It hurts the trees."

Though Brenner began to remember, he remained unaware he was dreaming. He turned to Lily, who's eyes were now wet, and began, "Lily Sullivan… or Miles, I have loved you for what feels like a lifetime. Your vow—you *were* all those things to me, Lily. You were my defender, my pride, my energy, my pursuer, my world, and my savior. When my cup was empty, you filled it. Was it always perfect? No, but I think that's the beauty of marriage. It's the perfect imperfection that constitutes love. Anyone can love another in a vacuum, where the world doesn't trip you or push you down. You loved me through the thick and thin of life. I'm sorry that I was distant in the end. There were things I was frustrated by in our relationship and instead of meaningful discussions with you or a therapist, I let them rot and stink up our marriage. Yet, you continued to love. You promised me that you would love me and only me until the end of your life. Lily Miles, you accomplished that." Brenner started to cry. "You don't have to love me anymore. It's finished, baby."

Lily disappeared and Brenner suddenly awoke.

Chapter 17

Brenner let himself come to slowly, reflecting on his dream and, more importantly, the sense of mournful peace that accompanied it. Squirrels scampered along the ground somewhere behind the shelter and birds began welcoming the new day, singing to each other their sweet melodies. For a moment, Brenner wished that he could be a songbird waking up in the safety of the canopy high above, whistling to his friends and reveling in the arrival of the sun, concerns of love and heartbreak whisked away in the gentle morning breeze. But then he supposed that birds could experience broken hearts as well. The thought almost made him regret his mornings spent duck hunting, knowing that most ducks mate for life. Had he put mallards, wigeon, and teal through the same hell he endured?

Soon, the radiant light of day bathed the inside of the shelter and awoke his companion. Sam, to Brenner's joy, rose to her feet and limped in a slow circle before sniffing the pocket of her owner's backpack that contained her breakfast, whining gently. She turned and looked at him, making him first smile when he saw a brightness in her eyes, but then frown when he looked at her right hindlimb, held up close to her body in pain. Dried blood was still caked in her fur, hiding the mottled black and brown speckles.

"Alright, baby girl, let's get you some food. We have a big day." Sam ferociously attacked the food in her bowl like she had never eaten before, not even noticing the three cephalexin capsules. Brenner gave her a second helping when she looked dissatisfied with the initial amount.

Almost out of food himself, and unwilling to spend time cooking, Brenner ate a handful of jerky, promising himself he'd never eat it again after they got back to civilization, and began packing up camp. Since no tent needed stowing, it only took a few minutes to gather his belongings. When his backpack was strapped to him, he said a short prayer for his dog, that she would be able to make the journey, and that they would be successful in finding the trail again.

He pulled out the handheld GPS that was stowed in a small mesh pocket on the waistband of his backpack. His heart began to race when it wouldn't turn on. He depressed the button for thirty seconds straight—still nothing. Finally, he was able to get it to show the "empty battery" symbol. When turned off, this specific device would last several months between charges, and he had charged it completely before embarking on his trip. Something—or someone—had fried it.

"Okay then," he said, defeated, trying not to panic, "I guess we'll just start walking that way."

Rather than barreling through the woods as she had on other mornings of their journey, Samantha hobbled next to Brenner, looking up to him for confidence and direction, hopping along on her three legs far better than he would have managed on one but still far from the bounding, happy hound she'd been before. The two of them trudged along slowly, but steadily, in the direction Brenner guessed they had come from two nights before. His plan was to find the trail and immediately make their way to the nearby Nantahala Whitewater Center, back to the safety of other people, civilization, and, hopefully, freedom from the spirit in the woods. After a veterinary hospital his second stop was going to be at a church.

Brenner and Sam put hill after hill in their rearview mirror, some small and some grand, pausing at prominent rises to check the horizon and confirm they were still generally walking northeast. Fortunately, most of this mountain was covered by eastern white pines, rather than hardwoods, meaning brush was kept to a minimum by a heavy blanketing of needles. It also allowed them to walk quietly, something Brenner found comforting. He hoped their passing would go unnoticed.

"When we get home, I'm going to have to do something for you, Sam," Brenner said, watching his dog hop on three legs, occasionally stumbling. "You'll have to be brave. When you are healed, I'll take you shopping and you can get a new bed, new toys, new treats…" Her ears twitched at hearing the last word and she looked up at him. "Anything for food, huh?" *Dogs and cats are tripods with a spare*, he told himself, echoing his orthopedic surgery professor from veterinary school.

Brenner first started to become concerned when the sun reached its climax in the sky with still no sign of the Appalachian Trail. *There's no way we ran this far, especially with how Sam was…*

Being lost in the mountains is a feeling only one who has experienced it can understand. At first you deny it. "I'm not lost. I know where to go," you say as you venture further and further away from the familiar. You start to look around and realize nothing in your setting is recognizable. Then suddenly, at a different time for each person, the feeling hits you like a freight train. You didn't notice the increase of your heart rate until all the sudden it's beating faster than you thought possible. Adrenaline is dumped into your bloodstream, and you begin to feel panic and dread. Your movements become erratic, almost twitchy. Your eyes bounce back and forth from different objects in your surroundings, hoping to find something they know. You may turn in several circles as you attempt to figure out where you are. Unless you were keenly aware of the horizon before losing your way, the circles you just turned ensure that you become confused, now questioning the very direction of the path you just walked. Now is the time for expletives and prayers. You're lost.

Brenner, in his naivety, hoped finding the trail would be easy, if he walked in a straight line for long enough, sure that he would find a point of intersection. But now, as he began to understand that he was truly lost, he realized that he could perhaps be merely paralleling the trail, if it had taken a sharp northward turn, or even meandered back to the east. "Well, shit," he said quietly, looking at Sam, knowing he had already asked much of her that day. Her energy was not without limit, and he worried he would exhaust it if they pressed forward. He put his hands on his knees and shouted, "Goddamnit!"

As much as he didn't want to erase their progress, he decided they needed to try to retrace their steps from the day and see if they would have more luck looking for signs of their passing the night of Sam's injury. "I'm sorry, girl. I'm failing you." Brenner cried as he redirected his dog back in the direction they had come from.

They walked for an hour back to the southwest, unsure if they were walking along a familiar path or not. The trees all looked the same to him. Full panic set in when Brenner and Sam mounted a small ridgeline that he was sure he had no memory of. He collapsed to his knees and let his forehead come to rest on the soft moss underneath him. "I could use a little help!" He prayed hopelessly. "Please…" Brenner wept.

His attention was pulled from self-pity when Sam barked at something behind him. With closed eyes, Brenner heard the wingbeat of a bird flying in a circle above them. *The mockingbird.*

His heart filled with warmth and hope when he saw the creature beckoning them to follow. As soon as he made eye contact, the bird flew due south. Brenner and Sam followed. At times, the hound had difficulty keeping up, but the bird would land on a limb and wait for them. Once Sam had caught her breath it would take flight again. This continued for two hours.

At long last, the mockingbird landed on the ground and began bouncing in circles, squawking. Brenner ran over to the bird and immediately noticed the ground—blood, a lot of blood. "Sam, look! We were here!" He turned around, ecstatic, and looked for the mockingbird, but it had flown away. "Thank you!" he shouted through the trees. It was easy to follow the trail now that they had one. Every ten to twenty feet, Brenner found new dried blood, only partially washed away from the passing showers the preceding day. Additionally, he would find footprints and Sam's tracks.

The two of them methodically pressed forward towards their original campsite, and more importantly, the trail. The young vet felt his energy sapped away from the day of panicked hiking. He watched as Samantha had also slowed down tremendously, pausing to breathe heavily every few hundred feet. Whether it was the recognition of the surroundings or just a feeling, Brenner began to know they were approaching the campsite. When the hound finally refused to move any farther, Brenner picked her up and carried her the last quarter mile. At last, they broke through a tree line and stumbled upon the back edge of the humble clearing. The tent was empty, and the unzipped door fluttered softly in the breeze. There was no sign of the creature. Brenner sat Sam in the tent and sighed.

As tired as she was, Sam readily ate dinner, albeit from a position of lying down. "We can't go any further," he mumbled perhaps to his dog and perhaps to himself. The last thing Brenner wanted was to spend another night out there, especially here, but he had no choice. Neither one of them had energy left to hike and it was still several miles to the safety of the road. Meanwhile, the sun sank lower and lower in the sky. "At least the tent is already set up."

But it may come back.

When Sam finished eating, Brenner patted her on the head and said softly, "Just stay here and sleep. Dad has work to do."

At this point, his best guess as to what was haunting him was a demon pretending to be Lily. He never believed in angels, demons, or spirits of any type, but then again, he would never have believed any of the things that had happened during the last week. One thing was certain: that creature was NOT Lily, and it meant to harm them. In his dream the night before, Brenner had at long last made peace with Lily's death. As much as he had hoped, there was no bringing her back and there was no option of staying with *her*. It was done. Over. It was time to move on.

The question that Brenner now considered was what to do in the event the thing came back before they could leave the trail, and specifically, what to do if it returned that night while they slept in the tent. He racked his brain and tried to remember every horror movie he'd ever watched that involved demons or ghosts. Holy water, exorcisms, catholic priests. "Ugh," he moaned, as he paced back and forth next to the stone fire ring. He finally sat down, feeling fresh exhaustion, both mental and physical.

As his eyes began to glaze while staring in the direction of the bed of coals, he noticed something shimmering and blinked a couple of times to clear his vision. In disbelief, he crawled towards the ring, stopping short with mouth agape. It was Lily's locket. How? He reached into the ring to grasp the small circle of silver. The moment his fingers contacted the cool metal, the world turned black at his periphery, and he was thrust into a deep vision.

His entire journey flashed before his eyes, starting with the original dream of the clearing in the woods. He saw Lily lying in their bed in South Carolina, looking into his eyes. The crash of balls and Dr. Johnson holding a pool cue in one hand and a glass of whisky in the other. The store clerk, Tallulah Gorge, and the thunderstorm on his first day hiking. Next, he saw Sticks holding out the bag of mushrooms, smiling. Colors shifted and Brenner saw ethereal reflections of his trip. He once again ran from the spirit in the woods to find the stone shelter, walking with Rami. Next, Rami was casting a fly to the bank of a small stream. Lily then appeared and begged Brenner to stay with her in the woods and abandon his friend. The field of vision flipped again, and Brenner saw himself in the bar with Hope. His stomach fluttered when he kissed her outside his motel room. Rising from the ground and taking Hope's place was Lily, with fire in her eyes. She reached towards him and shrieked, causing Brenner to turn and run. Long, effortful strides struggled to put ground between him and the ghost. He tripped on a root and found himself on the trail near the twisting tree at Bly Gap. In front of him, rather than Lily, stood Rami, Sticks, and Hope.

At the same time the three of them opened their mouths and said in unison, "Your name, Brenner… It means 'burn'!"

Brenner's eyes snapped open, and he breathed heavily. The locket was gone, but he knew what he had to do. In the next few minutes Brenner came up with a plan that started with making sure the fire had fresh embers that would last all night. He ignored the worry that a fire would attract the demon and began setting a small pile of sticks ablaze in the middle of the ring. He continued stoking and adding wood until a healthy fire burned. Next, he found the bottle of lighter fluid he'd bought in Franklin and set it in the tent near where he would be sleeping, in a place easily accessible in the dark. Lastly, Brenner set to stacking dead brush and logs from around the campsite inside of the tent, all around the edges. He added numerous handfuls of pine straw atop the stacks of logs. Once satisfied, he returned to continue maintaining the fire.

For the plan to work, he would have to trick it into going inside the tent. He was worried after the other night that it would harm them immediately, but he hoped and prayed he knew exactly what it wanted and would be able to use that against it. The plan was good but could be derailed with ease if it caught on. Brenner began to feel excitement, realizing he and Sam might not only be able to escape, but rid themselves of this demon forever. A return to normal life felt attainable for the first time in a while.

As the sun dipped below the horizon, a heavy, ominous feeling settled in Brenner's chest—the kind that comes before a storm.

He pushed down the fear that kept trying to rise in his gut, forcing his focus onto his goal. More than that, his motivation. Protecting Sam. This thing had hurt his dog. And now, he would destroy it—send it back to whatever hell had cast it out.

Little swirls of smoke curled from the flames as they licked hungrily at the fresh oak limbs. Without realizing it, Brenner was glowering into the fire, his jaw clenched tight.

When night was truly dark, he rose and walked to the tent. Once inside, he positioned the zipper so the door was left slightly open—easy to slip through, if needed. Then he crawled into his sleeping bag, nestling down beside his sleeping dog, surrounded by stacks of wood and brush.

Though he had planned on staying awake all night, sleep ensnared him around three in the morning. Brenner enjoyed a dreamless sleep, requiring no further memories or visions for motivation. His rest was cut short a little over two hours later.

Chapter 18

Can memories be willfully destroyed? They can be lost to the dense accumulation of time, finally relegated to the past when enough new memories have accumulated over top of them. Maybe a sound or a smell will awaken some piece of them, making them momentarily recollectable, before being sucked back into the vacuum. Eventually, the substance of the memory dissolves entirely and then somehow the moment no longer exists in any timeframe. Absent from the mind and unable to be remembered, the memory may never have existed in the first place. Such is how we forget. But can a memory be destroyed?

Brenner abruptly sat up when he noticed the disturbance outside the tent. He placed a hand on Sam to keep her from making any noise. It was still dark outside, but the air had an eerie glow. As he heard soft footsteps approaching the tent, the glow grew brighter and brighter. *It's time.* Brenner's stomach clenched and he began to perspire as he reached for the bottle of lighter fluid. After removing the cap, he inverted the bottle and began drenching the wood and brush that lined the tent, evenly dispersing the clear liquid until the bottle was empty. He held his breath and clinched his eyes tightly as he slowly began to unzip the door of the tent. In response, the light stopped moving and footsteps ceased.

"Okay, girl, let's go," Brenner said, turning back to Sam, who now stood right behind him. He exited the tent and locked eyes with Lily, who stood silently and still ten feet from him. Once Sam had also cleared the doorway, he beckoned her to the woods on the far side of the campsite, away from the spirit. The hound needed no encouragement to put distance between herself and the evil mockery of her mom, remembering their last interaction, and eagerly hobbled away from the tent.

Lily looked back and forth from dog to owner and finally said, "You came back." Her voice seemed calm and almost friendly, but Brenner saw death in her eyes. He thought of the words he had rehearsed.

"Truthfully, we couldn't make it very far after I saved Sam."

"It was an accident," Lily said, through tight lips.

Relax, you can do it. "But, if you want to know the truth," he paused when Lily took another step towards him, "I have been thinking about everything you've said."

Lily raised her eyebrows. "What have you been thinking about, sweetie?"

"I'm not sure I know how to exist without you," he lied. "In fact, I'm not certain I even *want* to live without you. I've thought all this time that I would heal by moving on, but I think I've come to realize that there is no healing. You're mine and I'm yours, in this life or whatever life there is after."

"Baby," Lily said softly, coming and sitting next to him. "This is what you truly want?"

Brenner concealed a violent shudder by coughing. "It is. I now understand this whole time you were trying to make a way for us to be together forever. Since I'm alive and you're not…"

Lily laid a cold hand atop Brenner's wrist and looked at him with longing eyes. "You understand now what has to be done?"

"I do."

Lily extended her arms and held Brenner's hands, this time giving no memory. They stood there in the forest and looked deeply into each other's eyes. It became so quiet that Brenner could hear his heart beating softly in his ears. For a moment, he thought he could even hear Lily's heart beating for him. *Lub dub, lub dub, lub dub…*

A seed of doubt somewhere deep in Brenner's soul cracked open from one end and a small shoot sprouted upward, growing with rapidity towards the gradient of transition between subconscious and conscious. He felt it push through the boundary and extend towards his heart and mind. Suddenly,

Brenner questioned everything, the fortress of resolve breaking apart one stone at a time. His legs began to shake as his mind started pivoting. *Lily.*

A tear streaked down Brenner's face, signifying that Lily had won. He was hers. She opened her mouth and spoke. "This will be easy, as you've already prepared the tent for yourself."

Brenner heard what she said, but was stuck in a trance-like state, mind accepting his fate.

"Come on, sweetie, I'll be right outside waiting for you." She pulled on his hands and started leading him towards the tent. He followed with short, methodical steps, inching closer and closer to a fate he had so strongly rejected just minutes before. Lily never broke eye contact with her husband, leading him as much with her eyes as with her touch. When they approached the tent, she folded back the door and whispered, "I'll love you forever, Brenner Miles, and forever starts now."

Brenner watched in helpless horror, trapped in his own mind, as he lifted his left leg and placed his foot inside the tent. At that moment, Lily broke eye contact and shrieked, echoing a ghastly sound into the morning air. Brenner suddenly snapped from his trance, pulled his leg forcefully out of the tent, and looked at the sky, in the direction of the demon's gaze. The mockingbird.

The small bird was flying in a steep dive from the heavens, shouting, "Now Brenner! Do it now!"

Within seconds the mockingbird contacted the spirit's face and proceeded to peck at its eyes, flying in frenzied circles around it. It spun around back and forth, swatting in the air, trying to grab the bird. Brenner ran to the firepit to grab an ember but tripped over a stone and fell to his hands and knees. Sam started howling from the woods, causing Brenner to look back and watch as the creature finally made firm contact with the mockingbird, sending its broken body to crash to the ground behind the tent. It weakly flapped and twitched and looked to Brenner.

Knowing his distraction was spent, he charged at the creature with the fullness of accumulated rage and shoved it backward, into the tent. As it fell away from him, he shouted, "This is for Sam!"

It flew backwards through the air, seemingly in slow motion, arms extended towards Brenner, and crashed down on top of the tent, bouncing off the piled wood below. Brenner ran to the fire and reached towards the embers with bare hands. He shouted in pain when he grabbed several of the largest coals, still red from the night before. His skin sizzled and burned as he whipped around to see the creature entangled in the tent poles still struggling to rise sightless. He threw the embers onto the middle of the tent, adjacent to the spirit. Small flames started rising around them. Brenner returned and grasped several more from the fire, throwing them to the unburning side.

The image of Lily started screaming as its leg caught fire. Within seconds, the lighter fluid-soaked wood ignited and formed a blue inferno that extended to every corner of the tent. The demon struggled to rise to its feet, but it was too late and its whole body began to burn. It fell back to its knees and threw her its back, releasing a guttural, evil moan into the mountain air, causing all nearby birds and creatures to flee. The trees that circled the edge of the campsite started to groan as well, louder, and louder, until the entire forest was calling out in pain. The bark of two nearby pines split open, starting at the base of the trunks, and spiraling upwards towards their branches. Then, suddenly, the closest tree exploded, sending shards of wood in every direction.

Brenner collapsed onto his back and grasped his ears, which burned intensely at the sound of the cries. With his head to the side, still watching the tent, Brenner saw a shape in the middle of the fire. It was darker than black, as if it sucked in the light around it. At first it was shaped like Lily, but soon the image of his wife was shed, and the beast was left in its naked form. Brenner watched in horror as wings unfurled from its back, also catching fire. Its mouth was still open and screaming and Brenner saw row after row of gnarled, elongated teeth. Instead of a nose, the spirit only had a large hole and steam poured from it and rose with the flames. When it finally stopped screaming, the spirit lowered its head and looked at Brenner with yellow, glowing eyes, layered thick with hatred and death. It raised a long, black arm and pointed at Brenner, who was unable to move.

A strong breeze from every direction pulled leaves and air into the fire towards the creature. The whole forest seemed to move towards the dying evil. At once the breeze stopped and an unnatural decrescendo of sound reached the point of silence. An opening in the sky above the tent shone light down at the beast, causing it to start melting into the Earth through another hole that had opened directly below the flames. Brenner watched as the demon was pulled out of this world and banished back to the hell whence it came.

The chasms closed and the fire extinguished itself, leaving Brenner, Sam, and the dying mockingbird in the woods alone, free from evil.

With the spirit gone, Brenner's energy returned, and he was able to rise. He groaned as his burned hands pushed him up from the dirt, but he tried his best to ignore the pain. Once on his feet he ran to the bird. However, when he passed the smoking tent and looked to the ground he stopped in his tracks and his stomach turned over. In place of the mockingbird lay Rami, broken and barely breathing.

"Rami!" he shouted as he ran to his friend's side, falling next to him on the dirt and throwing his arms around him.

"You did it," Rami said softly, before a short coughing fit. He winced and held his belly, tears welling up in his eyes.

"It was you the whole time," Brenner whispered in disbelief.

Rami nodded.

"I don't understand. Who are you, really?"

Rami responded weakly, "I may have made an understatement when I said I'd grown up in the church." He watched Brenner try to process what he was saying. "As I'm sure you've realized by now, that *thing* wasn't Lily. When they realized it was trying to harm you, they sent me to help..."

"Who sent you?" After a moment of silence, Brenner guessed, "God? God sent you?"

"And..." Rami was growing weaker by the second but was finally able to produce a second name. "Lily."

Brenner started crying and laid his forehead down on Rami's chest. "Thank you, Rami. I'm so sorry I left you—abandoned you. I felt powerless." They sat like this for many moments and Brenner listened to the sounds of the new day mixed with Rami's struggled breathing. The air seemed lighter than it had in a long time and Brenner was breathing freely once more. The birds even seemed happier in their songs; happy their home was rid of the ghastly presence. When Brenner had gathered his thoughts, head still resting on his friend, he said, "Tell Lily thank you for me." He felt a friendly, acknowledging pat on his back.

When he lifted his head, Rami was no longer there underneath him. A large stone had taken his place, and the sun broke through the canopy, illuminating the spot on the forest floor with a bright, warm, morning ray. Brenner rose to his feet and looked at Sam, who had walked over to him, still holding her right hindlimb painfully off the ground. "Let's go home, girl."

Chapter 19

The sound of a beeping pulse oximetry device and the occasional inflation of a blood pressure cuff filled the small surgical suite. Brenner leaned against the far wall and watched Dr. Johnson disarticulate Sam's femur from her pelvis. It was late Friday evening. Brenner called ahead when he left the mountains, and Ben was eager to meet him at the clinic when he heard about Sam. He had considered rushing her to an emergency clinic that was closer to the trail, but he knew another practice wouldn't let him be by her side during the procedure. If something happened to her, he wouldn't be able to forgive himself for being in another room.

"She's lucky, you know," Ben said, looking up from the surgical field. "Even if she didn't bleed out, spending multiple days in the woods with this kind of wound… Sam could have easily become septic."

"Oh, believe me, I know." Brenner frowned.

"You did a good job, Brenner. She'd be dead if it weren't

for you. I don't know if I would have been so calm." Ben cut through the ligament of the head of the femur and pulled Sam's dying leg from her body and set it on the mayo stand behind him. "It never ceases to amaze me how nasty barbed wire wounds can be."

Brenner's stomach turned over. *Barbed wire. If only they really knew…*

"Hey Ben," he said, causing the latter to look at him again. "I'm ready to come back to work."

"Are you sure? I don't want you to come back too soon and there is no reason to rush healing. Your spot will be here no matter how long it takes." He looked at Brenner's burned hands, which he had just bandaged moments before. "And what about those?"

"I can just do rooms until they scar over. I'll go to the doctor tomorrow. Seriously Ben, I'm ready. I found what I needed. I've healed. I felt like my life didn't have purpose while I was gone. At this point, I just need to work. I miss my clients, and I miss you guys."

"Well, in that case, how about Monday?" Ben smiled.

"Sounds like a plan."

Brenner and Ben sat together in the office sharing beers while Sam recovered from anesthesia, which took about three hours. Brenner decided he wouldn't tell anyone about Rami, the mockingbird, or the spirit, for fear of making other people worried about his mental health. He had realized that if someone else told him the same story, he would never believe them. Instead, he told Ben about Sticks and the mushrooms.

Ben caught his breath after laughing, "You're insane, you know. First of all, how could you trust a stranger in the woods like that? And eating half of them? It's a miracle you made it off the trail."

"You have no idea," Brenner chuckled.

"Well good morning, Samantha. You're looking a little brighter," Ben said, looking at the three-legged hound stirring on the quilt at their feet.

"Thanks again, Ben. I owe you."

"You owe me nothing. We'll keep you out of surgery until your hands are healed." He pointed at the counter behind Brenner, "Her drugs are all filled and over there. I'm going to go home and get some sleep. Lock up when you guys leave."

"Will do. See you Monday."

***

Back home, after showering and setting up a spot for Sam, Brenner finally climbed into his own bed, exhaling as he felt the cool, clean sheets brush against his legs and torso. He tried to fall asleep but became restless. A few minutes passed and Brenner realized trying to sleep would be futile, so he opened the drawer of his nightstand and found the Polaroid of Lily that had been in there since the early days of their dating relationship. He smiled when he saw her kind eyes and let himself remember all the things he loved about her. He ran his thumb over her hair and whispered, "Thank you."

Still unable to sleep, Brenner got out of bed and started walking towards the door of the bedroom, pausing to make sure Sam was still sleeping. He walked to the kitchen and pulled his journal out of the backpack that still sat by the door. It felt unnaturally heavy in his hand and, instead of opening it, he walked straight to the trashcan and threw it away. He then walked to the bookshelf and found a journal that hadn't been used yet, taking it with him back to the bedroom. Once in bed, he opened the first page and started writing, "Lily and the Mockingbird…"

At some time around four in the morning, sleep finally caught up with him and Brenner drifted into a heavy, dreamless sleep, one that had been due for weeks. Sam slept heavily as well, though her sleep was not dreamless. She dreamt of Brenner.

The two rose at eleven the next morning and went to sit in the living room, Brenner drinking a strong cup of coffee with Sam at his feet. The former sighed and shifted again in his chair, dealing with some internal battle. He looked at Sam and then out the window. The day looked warm and bright, with not a single cloud in the sky. When he finished his coffee, Brenner walked into the backyard with Sam and enjoyed the feeling of the sun on his shirtless skin. He closed his eyes and nodded before pulling his phone out of his pocket and dialing. After two rings, a soft voice answered, "Hello?"

"Hey Hope. It's me, Brenner."

Made in the USA
Coppell, TX
13 January 2026

69124856R10173